OFF SIDES

AN ENEMIES TO LOVERS, ATHLETE/COACH ROMANCE

WILLOW BAY
BOOK 4

ELLA KADE

PHOTOGRAPHY BY
XRAM RAGDE

OFF SIDES

Join Ella's mailing list to be the first to know of new releases, free books, sales, and other giveaways!

https://www.harlowandellasromance.com/newsletter

I never thought I'd have to start over—let alone in my senior year of college.

Without my twin brother and my best friend, my life fell apart.

Now I was finally healthy and ready to meet my new team. That was until I saw who the assistant coach was. What was my ex, pro-soccer-playing boyfriend doing in Willow Springs? You know what? I didn't care. He dropped me like yesterday's garbage after he told me nothing would break us apart—not even an ocean.

He was a liar.

When I took the job as assistant coach, I never thought I'd see Danica Francisco. I knew her brother lived here, but not her. Why wasn't she three hours away?

I was finally getting my life back on track after what I thought was the worst time of my life. Except now, I was thinking taking this job was the worst decision I'd ever made besides cutting Danica out of my life.

Too bad she looks like she wants to kill me and put my body through a wood chipper every time she looks at me.

How was I going to survive being so close to her and yet so far away?

ONE
DANICA

"WELCOME to Willow 'Bad Things Happen Here' Bay," Oz greeted me as he walked through the room.

Wow.

"What's up your butt this morning?" I mumbled through a bite of scrambled eggs Ford had made for me.

"I'm not ready for these early mornings," he grumbled.

"What you mean is you're not ready to get out of bed when my best friend is right beside you all nice and cozy against you."

He wrinkled his nose. "When you say it like that it sounds wrong." His face fell and he moved to sit beside me at the table. "Please don't tell me you have a problem with us being together?"

I couldn't stop the eye roll even if I tried. "Of course,

not. You know I love the two of you together. *Now*." I felt bad for even expressing that I thought my twin brother wasn't good enough for Lo in the past. There was no one better for her than him, and vice versa.

"Okay," he shook his head, and went back to the stove where he plated his food before returning. "You're okay, aren't you?" He eyed my plate of food.

"How can I turn down food when Ford is over here making me gourmet meals just to make sure that I eat?" Ford was going to be world famous one day with the way he cooked. He could make anything spectacular.

"Seriously, I don't know how you all ever agreed to let him move out, so I could live here."

Oz's brows turned into angry slants. "Because we love you."

"You love Ford too," I shot back. I wasn't sure why I was trying to pick a fight. Actually, I did. I was nervous about my first day of practice. It wasn't easy coming onto a team your senior year. It would be like I was a freshman in their eyes.

"Yes, but I didn't share a womb, nor do I have an unbreakable bond with him. No one is more important to me than you."

It was on the tip of my tongue to say that Lo was more important, but I didn't. She should be. Lo was who my brother was planning to spend the rest of his life with. And I knew it would make him feel guilty if I told him that fact. He'd lived with enough guilt over the years.

Fin shuffled into the room with his eyes barely open, and a long strand of black hair hanging in front of one eye. He didn't speak as he moved in front of the stove and made himself a plate.

"I need coffee," he grumbled as he sat down at the other end of the table.

"Don't we all," I answered back, forking a strawberry and popping it into my mouth.

"Do you have your gear ready? We can drop you off at the field on the way to practice."

Pushing my plate away, I stood. "Are you trying to practice with me for the day that you have to take your kid to kindergarten or something?"

Oz and Fin eyed my plate.

Well, too fucking bad. Maybe I would have eaten it all if I could have eaten in peace.

"Dani, you need to eat." Oz looked down at my plate and then back to me. "Especially since you're going to be practicing today."

"You don't have to tell me," I gritted out. "Why don't you worry about your own life, and let me try to navigate my own?"

"That's not fair," he shot back.

Maybe it wasn't, but I didn't need a constant

reminder of all the ways I'd fucked up while I was at UCLA by myself. I'd let too many of the wrong people get into my head, but now all I wanted was to be able to think for myself. I didn't need my brother, his friends, or my best friend constantly hovering over me to tally up my daily intake of calories.

Stabbing one last piece of egg, I shoved it in my mouth and ate it while I glared at Oz. I turned my gaze to Fin only to see he was looking at his phone. At least, his attention wasn't on me. "There. Are you happy?"

"Yeah, I'm happy," Oz barked out as he backed up his chair, making the legs squeak across the floor. "We're leaving in ten. If you want a ride, be ready by then." He turned and went back to his bedroom that he shared with Lo. I didn't move until I heard the soft click of the door.

"I don't know how you stand to be friends with him sometimes." That wasn't true. Oz was an amazing friend. Actually, I wasn't sure why he was friends with Fin. Fin was an asshole most of the time. He was better now that he had West in his life, but he was still an angry twenty-one-year-old who was likely to blow at the drop of a hat on most days.

"He's only worried about you. He doesn't want you to slip. We all feel that way." Fin said without looking up from his phone.

"Even you?"

He nodded, but that was all the response I got. I knew how difficult it was for men to express their feelings, and Fin was ten times worse. It made me feel special he was worried about me.

"Thanks." I scrapped off my food into the trashcan before I rinsed my plate and put it in the dishwasher. "I'm going to grab my bag."

He nodded again, but this time I could see the trace of a smile at the corner of his lips.

I was sitting on the field, by myself, as I listened to my new coach talk about how this was going to be the women's soccer team best year yet. They had a new coach, and he was going to work one on one with the offense. I didn't care. Not anymore. Willow Bay's soccer team wouldn't get me the attention I needed to make it to the Olympics. It had always been a dream of mine, but that went up in smoke when I let a few choice words from my previous coaches influence me into thinking I'd be a better player and person if I lost weight. I trained more than I ever had in my life and barely ate my junior year of college.

And that was how I ended up here.

Living with my brother. Which was a thousand times

better than having to live back at home with my parents. They would have smothered me to death by now. Oz and Lo had only slightly snuffed out my flame since I'd been here over the summer.

A tall, lean man, with golden skin that made every woman want to lick every single inch of it, walked toward us. All eyes moved from Coach Parker to the lithe specimen that moved toward us.

I knew that body.

Intimately.

What the hell was he doing here?

This was my safe space. Away from coaches who didn't prioritize my well-being. Away from the memories of the man who broke my heart.

You know what? I didn't care. I was going to make his life a living hell just like he'd made mine when he ghosted me.

Declan Hart was going to regret ever stepping foot in Willow Bay.

TWO
DANICA

KEEPING MY HEAD DOWN, I shuffled out of the locker room and into the sunny morning. I hadn't made any friends. Not that I thought I would, and I didn't care. I wasn't here to have the time of my life. Willow Bay was the best option for me at the time, and I took it. Now I wasn't so sure living with my parents wouldn't be a better option with Declan here.

I spotted him out of the corner of my eye, but I kept walking. I was headed to the football stadium to get a lift home. If they weren't done with practice, I would happily kick back and watch them. There wasn't much better than a bunch of hot guys in tight pants showing off their asses.

Guilt washed through me at not attending even one of their football games when Oz had come to as many of mine as he could the last three years. I was a shit sister, but I vowed from here on out, I would be better.

"Danica, wait," Declan ordered in an irritated tone as he pushed off the wall.

With my gaze focused on the pavement, I kept moving. I had nothing to say to my ex. I could cut him off just as he'd done to me.

Gripping me by my upper arm, he pulled me back nearly tripping me. "Let go," I hissed out. When he kept his large hand wrapped around my bicep, I finally made eye contact. I didn't let his sad brown eyes affect me. Not anymore. Instead, I gritted my teeth and tried to keep my voice quiet. I didn't need attention brought to the fact that I was talking to the assistant coach. Rumors would be swirling around the field by the time I stepped foot on it tomorrow morning. "Now."

Dropping his hand like I just burned him, Declan stepped back. The muscle in his jaw twitched. "What are you doing here?"

"I think it's obvious why I'm here. What are you doing here?" I shot his question back at him.

"I was here first," he said like a petulant three-year-old.

"Well, goodie for you, but I'm here to stay. If you don't like it, you can leave."

He scoffed like what I'd just said was the most

ridiculous thing he'd ever heard when only seconds before he wanted me to leave.

His eyes raked over my thin frame. "What happened to you?"

"I could ask you the same question, but I don't give a shit, so I won't bother. I'm none of your concern now. You focus on your job, and I'll focus on my playing. I'll respect you on the field if you give me the same courtesy, but outside of that, I don't want to see your face or hear your voice." Without waiting for him to respond, I shot him the bird before I resumed my quest for hot guys in tight pants.

Having Declan here was going to be a problem. I could already feel unease growing inside of me. It started in my stomach and inched up my throat making it nearly impossible to swallow the water I tried to sip as I walked in the hot sun. I couldn't let one asshole ruin my recovery. If I was even recovered at all. It had only been a few short months. I was still too skinny. Even *he* saw it. Everyone saw it.

I tried to put on a sunny smile as I walked into the stadium toward the bleachers, knowing all eyes were on me. I didn't care about people watching me. I was used to it after playing soccer for years. What I cared about was how I came across to Oz, Fin, West, and Ford. They'd be on me like a heart attack if they thought something was wrong.

And it was wrong.

All wrong.

And I wasn't sure how to right it.

Sitting on the bleachers, I set my duffle bag beside me and got comfortable. I wasn't sure how long their practice would be. Ours was short which didn't bode well for the team. I was used to three to four hours every day, or I used to be. Ours had barely lasted an hour. Maybe it was because it was the first practice, but I had a feeling it said more about how it wasn't a top-notch team.

The guys probably had at least an hour left of theirs. I was slightly disappointed they didn't have their football pants on, but since most of them were shirtless, I couldn't complain. Ninety percent of the team was ripped. Seriously, they needed to have a Willow Bay football calendar they were so hot.

I wasn't sure what it said about me that I got all hot and bothered as I watched them practice. Their bodies slamming into one another and sweat making every ridge and muscle glisten. I was going to have to find a little me time once I got home. It wasn't easy to masturbate in a house with extremely thin walls when your brother was right next door. Nor was it easy to hear him banging my best friend. At the rate they were going, they were going to need to buy me a new pair of headphones before Thanksgiving.

"Hey, are you okay?" Oz stood before me blocking the sun and my view. When had he gotten here?

"Yeah, I'm fine."

"Practice go alright?" He shifted, his eyes locked on mine. "I thought for sure we'd be waiting on you."

I didn't want to get into here, and I knew I had to tell Oz. He already knew something was up, and it wouldn't do me any good to bottle it up.

"Why don't you go get cleaned up, and I'll tell you on the way home?" I leaned back and looked at the helmet that hung from his fingertips.

One blond brow rose. "Yeah?"

"Promise. Now go get your stinky self, cleaned up. You won't be able to get within ten feet of my best friend smelling like that."

He gave me a lopsided smile, and started walking backwards. "Thanks for looking out for me."

"Always," I promised. I gathered my things and followed him down the bleachers. "I'll meet you at the car."

"Are you sure everything's okay?"

"I'll tell you in a few." Pushing up on my toes, I wrapped my arms around his neck and hugged my brother before stepping back. Giving him my best smile,

I watched him head into the locker room. Every few steps he looked over his shoulder at me. Yeah, I wasn't fooling him.

"So, what's going on?"

"Wow," I laughed shakily. "I'm surprised you actually made it until we were out of the parking lot."

Fin eyed me through the rearview mirror with furrowed brows. Always so serious. "What's going on?"

"That's what I'm trying to find out. Did you see when she showed up to practice?"

West shook his head in front of me. When he was on the field, he was one hundred and ten percent focused on what he was doing, and it was paying off. There was talk he was going to be drafted into the NFL, and I was so happy for him. At least one of us would get to follow their dream.

"What happened?" Fin barked.

It was sweet the asshole cared. He was like a brother to me—a much grumpier brother, but a brother all the same since Oz and Fin had been best friends for so long.

Crossing my arms over my chest, I looked out the window. "You'll never guess who the new assistant coach is for the women's team."

West turned around to look at me. His green eyes lit up. "Beckham."

I cracked a smile. "You think I'd be sitting in this car if he was anywhere in the vicinity?"

He shrugged and turned back around.

Oz placed his hand on my leg and gave it a squeeze. "Who?"

"Fucking Declan."

I still couldn't believe it. Why here? Why wasn't he still playing in Spain?

"Are you fucking shitting me? Did he follow you here?" Oz growled out.

I shrugged because I had no clue and didn't really want to think about it. Declan ghosted me. I hadn't heard a single word from him in over a year, and that hurt. I thought he loved me, but I was stupid and naïve. How on this Earth would we have made a relationship work with him in Spain playing soccer with women throwing themselves at him day and night while I was still in college? I didn't know, but I thought it could work. Until it didn't.

Now he was here, and I wanted to ruin him the way he ruined me. If I hadn't felt like something was wrong with me then maybe I wouldn't have listened to my coaches when they told me I needed to lose weight. And then maybe I wouldn't have starved myself to the point of needing professional help.

I wasn't sure I'd ever be the same again.

Body or soul.

"We can kick his ass if that will make you feel better," Fin threw out from the driver seat.

"No, we won't," West spoke up. "This isn't a student. He's staff. If he's touched, we'll be kicked out." West turned around to look at me. "Dani is a strong woman, and she doesn't need any of us coming to her rescue."

West sounded so sure about me. It was a good thing someone was because I wasn't. No, I wasn't going to have any one of them risk getting thrown out of college their last year over me. Still, it made me feel all warm inside that they cared enough to consider it.

Fin frowned at his boyfriend, but didn't say another word.

"I can talk to him if you want," Oz volunteered. "Threaten him a little."

That had me smiling.

"I'm good. At least for now. I'm going to do something to make his life miserable, but I haven't figured it out yet."

"Date someone else," Fin threw out there. He certainly was chatty this afternoon.

Fin's idea wasn't a bad one, but it felt like too much

work. The only place I'd likely see Declan was at practice and games, and that meant I'd have to have a guy come to those. I mean if some guy asked to meet up, I could always suggest after practice, but I seriously doubted that was going to happen. School hadn't even started yet, and the only people on campus were athletes. Declan would hate to see me with a big, beefy football player.

Hmmm. Maybe I could meet someone.

"I don't think that's a good idea. Aren't you supposed to be relationship free for—"

I threw my hand up between me and my brother. "I'm not going to date anyone, but I could pretend. I'd use one of you if he hadn't met you all already." I looked out the window and sighed. "I'll think of something else like kicking the ball into his balls or grinding my cleat into them."

"Damn, remind me not to piss you off," West laughed from the front.

With their support, maybe it wasn't such a bad idea that I came to live here. I had people I loved here who were watching out for me and cared for me.

"Is Ford coming to make dinner for us tonight?" Fin asked.

"Yeah, I think he and Xander are both coming. We've really got to get him to do meal prep. He can't keep coming over just to cook for us, and then go home."

"Why not?" Fin asked West.

"Because he's going to be dragging ass just as much as us especially when two a day practices start."

"But it won't be nearly as good," Fin complained.

West rolled his head to look at his boyfriend and shook his head. "Maybe not, but we should give him the option. He has a lot going on with trying to finish his culinary degree, football, and keeping it on the DL that he's dating a professor."

"I think the school would be more pissed off that he's living with the professor, but what do I know," Fin smirked.

"Alright, smart ass. Still let's give him a pass. Let him do meal prep or only cook for us so many times a week. We're all adults and can manage." My brother said to Fin before he looked at me. His blue eyes that matched my own scanned my face as if he wasn't sure I could manage. Hell, I wasn't sure if I could either. Still, I managed to smile.

"I'll be fine." I tried to assure him.

At least I hoped I would be.

THREE
DECLAN

FUCK SHE WAS BEAUTIFUL, and she hated me. Dani more than hated me. She loathed me. If she could set me on fire, I was sure she'd do it and never look back as I went up in flames.

True to her word, Dani gave the same respect she did Coach Parker. She listened to my instructions and did what I asked of her on the field, but once the whistle blew at the end of practice, I no longer existed. I could have tried to talk to her during practice, but that would be wrong. If I broke the code, she would retaliate. I saw it on her stubborn yet gorgeous face every time she looked at me.

I still hadn't figured out why she was here and not at UCLA. The only thing I knew was she had called Coach Parker saying she was moving here and asked if there was a spot on the team open. Parker would have dismissed half the team to get someone as talented as Dani, so it was a no brainer she let her on the team.

That still didn't explain why Dani left a team that could put her in the Olympic spotlight. Something wasn't right. Multiple somethings.

Danica had always been in top physical condition, now she had lost some of her muscle. She was too thin. Weaker than she used to be. Still, she was the best player on the team.

What the hell had happened to her?

I knew there was no way in hell she was going to tell me either.

Today I was leading practice. While Coach Parker was a sweet woman, she didn't know what it took to make a great team. Her practices were barely an hour long. These girls needed to run, weight train, add some yoga to keep them limber, and do drills. Obviously not all on the same day. Instead of an hour they needed to be here at least two to three hours a day. I guess that's why I was here. To whip them all into shape.

It didn't escape my notice that Dani kept herself away from the rest of the team except when they were scrimmaging. Like now. She hovered in the background. Maybe she was trying to stay away from me, but I didn't think so.

Coach Parker left earlier this morning for an appointment. I was surprised she left it all to me, but I was going to take advantage of the time and show these girls how it was done.

"Stassi," I called out one of the strikers. "I want you to take the ball from me."

"But…" her mouth hung open.

"Do it," I ordered. She was the weakest on the offense, and you were only as great as your weakest player. More time needed to be spent on her.

"Okay," she squeaked.

"Do it like I showed you." I jogged trying to make it easy for her, but she was having a hard time sweeping the ball from me. How was she even on the team?

I was distracted by how horrible Stassi was that I didn't realize my mistake until I made it. One second, I was making my way down the field and the next crippling pain shot through my leg. How had she managed to kick me in the back of my calf when she was to be going after the ball in front of me, I'll never know, but she kicked me *hard*.

Bile rose in my throat as I tried to hold in my scream of pain. God damn it. I was stuck frozen unable to move. I didn't even want to try to put weight on my leg afraid of what the damage was.

There was a cheer and Stassi was jumping up and down at the goal where no one was defending it.

I blew my whistle, and all eyes were on me. "Practice is over," I barked.

All the girls looked at me. Seriously, how had they not noticed what their shitty team player had done?

I stood as still as a statue without putting any pressure on my foot or leg until every last person was gone.

What the hell was I going to do if I was injured again?

It wasn't like I was playing, but it had taken me a long time to recover from my injury. I hadn't exactly been in the best headspace either. I wasn't sure where I'd be right now if it wasn't for my sister. If she hadn't demanded I move in with her I would be nothing but a lump on a couch somewhere wallowing in self-pity. I couldn't let that happen again. I'd finally bought my own place here, so I didn't feel like I was always intruding on Roxy and her boyfriend, Merrick.

"Are you okay?" Dani's sweet voice asked without venom this time. I was lucky to get two words out of her when I spoke to her, so for Dani to seek me out was something.

Swallowing the lump in my throat, I choked out the words I didn't mean. "Yeah, I'm fine."

"Is that why you've been standing in the same place

for the last ten minutes?" There was a pause and then she said softly. "You look *green*."

I had no doubt I probably was green. The pain was still searing up my calf. It felt as if it had been cut open. I'd glanced down and saw no outer wound to go along with the pain, just the panic bubbling up inside of me if I was indeed hurt again.

"I just need a few minutes, and then I'll be fine." I told her and myself trying to believe in the words that had just come out of my mouth.

"If you're sure." She didn't sound like she believed me. Hell, I didn't either.

My senses must have been attuned to everything. The second I heard the crunch of grass under her cleats I spoke. "Wait, Dani." I still hadn't looked at her. I couldn't. Unsure of what I'd see once our eyes met.

"What is it Declan?" She huffed. "I need to meet my brother and his friends."

Somehow, she already had a life here, and I had nothing but my sister. I didn't want this job, but what was I going to do? My career playing soccer was over. I thought coaching would be the next best thing. That was until Dani showed up on the team. I just had to get through this season. She'd be gone next year. Living her best life while I wallowed in my shitty existence.

Swallowing my pride, I opened my mouth. "Can you help me over to the bench?

Dani didn't speak. She let out a deep sigh and then she was standing at my side. The side I hadn't put any weight on yet.

The feel of her warm skin touching mine as she moved to put herself under my arm and then pressed the side of her body into mine had my skin buzzing. It had been too long since I'd last felt her. My dick instantly reacted to having her so close. Too bad he hadn't gotten the memo that she was no longer ours.

"Put your weight on me and let's get you over there." Her tone was bored. She didn't want to be anywhere near me, and I didn't blame her. If only I could have explained what was going on with me after I'd been injured. Maybe she would understand. But I couldn't. Hell, I was still bitter about that asshole ending my career just when it started.

"Okay," I groaned as I gave her as much weight as I felt she could take which wasn't much. Where was my strong girl?

"You can give me more." Dani wrapped her arm around my waist and took a step forward. I gave her more, but only because I had to. The fifty feet to the bench might as well have been three hundred with how long it took to get my ass over there. Dani was sweating and panting as she maneuvered to sit me down.

Only once my ass was on the hot metal did I meet her eyes, and I didn't like what I saw. They held pity in them. Exactly what I didn't want.

Breaking eye contact, I looked to the ground. "Can you hand me my bag?"

Without a word, she retrieved my bag and set it beside me. Why couldn't I talk to her? Tell her how sorry I was for never picking up the phone or answering any of her messages.

I felt her leave and only then did I dig into my bag and pull out my cellphone. I didn't want to call my sister and her boyfriend, but who else was I going to call? An ambulance? Not happening.

"Here." An ice pack was shoved into my empty hand. "Once you ice it, it should feel better." She moved to sit at the end of the bench just shy of where my leg extended. I watched as she chewed on the inside of her cheek for a long moment before she straightened her spine and took the ice pack from me. "Is it in the same place?"

"Yeah," I barely got out. Dani didn't know exactly where it was because she hadn't been there, but only because I hadn't let her.

Gingerly she lifted my shoe and placed the ice pack under my calf before guiding my foot back down.

"I wish I could hate you right now, but I can tell how much pain you're in and that's enough for now. I'm going to get out of here before my brother shows up and I have to stop him from beating the shit out of you."

"Thanks?" I cleared my throat trying to shake myself out of my Dani induced haze I was in from being in such close proximity. "Thanks for helping me and for keeping your brother away."

"It will only be this once. I still hate you, but it's no fun trying to ruin you when you're already down."

It was one thing to think, but a whole other to have her say it.

"Dani," a deep voice barked. For a split second I thought it might be her boyfriend until I spotted the blond hair and recognized her brother. Fin, West, and Ford walked in behind him and scowled at me. I was sure they all wanted to kick my ass. I didn't blame them. I wanted to kick my own ass for the way I ended things with Danica.

Dani looked from her brother to me and back again. "If the ice doesn't help, you should probably have a doctor take a look at it."

I nodded. My calf was feeling better, but I knew I needed to get in to see my doctor. My soleus muscle had torn where I'd had surgery on it before. There was no reason, even after being kicked in the same place, for me to be experiencing this much pain. I'd more than likely show up to practice tomorrow with crutches—if I could drive since it was my right leg.

Unable to do anything else, I watched her go wondering how I was going to get her back. Dani hated me, and it was going to take a miracle for her to even listen to me try to explain why I did what I did, let alone forgive me.

FOUR

DANICA

DECLAN WAS DEFINITELY MAKING it difficult to ruin his life when he wasn't showing up to practice. It had been a week since Stassi had clipped him in the leg. At first, I thought he wasn't showing up because of his precious pride, but seven days later and I was wondering just how injured he was.

Not that I cared.

Or maybe he took to heart my words and realized I would do everything in my power to ruin him. I just hadn't figured out how to. *Yet.*

"Is he bothering you?" Oz said in a quiet voice as we rode in the back of Fin's car on the way to practice.

"He hasn't been back," I muttered, clenching my fists.

"Then why the resting bitch face?" I could hear the humor in his voice, but I didn't care, it still pissed me off.

It wasn't fun to be the lonely, single person in a group who had found their people. Everyone surrounding me was shitting rainbows they were so happy all the time. Okay, maybe not Fin, but it was as close as he was ever going to get.

"Because how am I supposed to make his life miserable when he's not around." Maybe he'd be back today. It was the start of a brand-new week.

"What are you going to do?" Oz reached over and took my hand. "This isn't like you."

"Maybe this is the new me." I placed my other hand over his and looked toward the front of the car. "Fin, what would you do?"

His eyes flicked to mine then his best friend's before they went back on the road. "Kick his ass, but that isn't really an option for you." He hummed deep in his throat. He was really thinking about it. Normally I wasn't a bitch or devious, but I blamed Declan for my downfall, and I wanted him to fall over the cliff right along with me. Even if I had to push him.

"You could set him up and make it look like he's fucking one of the players." I saw the smile creep on his face. Fin might have had West to keep him settled, but I knew there was something deep down that was burning to be let loose.

"I like that idea." Leaning forward, I placed my hand

on his shoulder before I quickly moved to remove it. Fin's hand caught mine and tapped it once. That one gesture was like a big bear hug from him. "Now all he needs to do is show his face at practice."

"If you need more help let me know," Fin smirked.

West gave him a disapproving look from beside him, but didn't say anything. While he tamed the beast inside Fin, he knew sometimes it had to be let out every once in a while, and I would accept any help from the master.

Fin pulled up in front of the soccer field and put the car in park. The trunk popped indicating it was time for me to get out. I could drive myself, but everyone insisted we all ride together. It didn't matter if I had to wait on them or if they had to wait on me. We were a unit, and we'd do this until we couldn't.

Ice doused my insides at the thought that after this year, I wouldn't have this. It also hurt to know I missed three years of this while I was at UCLA. Why did I want to do my own thing when I would have the rest of my life once college was over to be by myself?

"I'll see you after practice." I waved after closing the trunk with my bag hooked on my shoulder.

I heard a couple of girls giggling as they walked by, but I paid them no attention. I still hadn't made any friends on the team not that I thought I would. Not to be conceited, but I was the team's best player, and with me here, it ruined the chance for my teammates to shine.

I rushed through the locker room, ready to get out on the field. When I was out there, I forgot everything else. That might have been a problem since if I kept doing drills, running, or anything really, I could go all day and not eat. That part of my disorder had not been trained out of me. That was why I had found it so easy to lose weight like my coaches wanted. It was a win-win situation. At least back then. Now I needed to be reminded to eat, so I didn't slip back into that dark hole.

To my surprise, Declan was on the field today. I hated that I wanted to know why he'd been gone. How could he have been that hurt from such a small side swipe? And how the hell didn't anyone else notice it?

We all moved to sit in a circle around our coaches to listen to the plan for the day and the week. A few of the girls were whispering and laughing, but I paid no attention to them. I'd found the girls here to be petty and snobby. It wasn't the first time I wished Lo played soccer, so I'd have someone on the field with me.

I barely listened as Coach Parker talked about being split up into groups of three to work on drills for the first hour. She mentioned something about Coach Hart pulling us aside to review our scores. I wasn't sure why they were going over our performance now and not the first day, but whatever. I already knew I'd have the highest score, so I didn't care.

It wasn't until we broke apart and Declan limped off to the side, I realized the girls had been laughing at him. It was also the first time I realized he didn't have his usual knee-high socks on. Well, they weren't his normal before he showed up in Willow Bay. He used to always wear ankle socks unless he was playing. I stared at his calf with the angry red scar slicing through it. Had he been hiding his scar from all of us this whole time?

"It's so gross," one of the girls said in a tone that had my hackles rising. I didn't know her name. Or any of their names unless they turned their backs to me and I saw it on their jerseys. It didn't matter. Even though I hated Declan they shouldn't make fun of him. Especially when it was one of them who made him like this. I knew the scar was old, but it was angry because of Stassi.

Pain flared in his chocolate eyes, and I lost my mind. Before I could blink, I was in front of her with my hands on my hips. "Why don't you go fuck off? Have you seriously never been injured playing? Oh right, probably not because you're usually sitting on the bench. Well, if you did, you'd know that shit happens, and you get hurt. You should never make fun of anyone for their scars. Inside or out."

She sputtered, but before she had a chance to retaliate

and for me to annihilate her, a strong arm was around my shoulders, pulling me back. Even without the familiar arm around me, I would have known who it was by his scent. I'd never been able to pinpoint what it was, but it was the manliest spicy scent that I'd ever encountered. It smelled like home and that pissed me off.

"Don't get kicked off the team for me," he muttered in my ear as he pulled me away from the situation.

"She's a bitch," I snarled.

"Perhaps, but it doesn't matter. I'll live." The deep, husky tone of his voice snapped me out of whatever stupor I was in. I extricated myself from his presence and stalked off to do my drills. Alone. There's no way in hell, I'd be joining the rest of the team today.

Stupidly I looked over my shoulder to see Declan looking at me with a lost puppy dog expression on his stupid handsome face. Damn him. He looked like I'd given him hope. Why hadn't I kept my mouth shut?

Because even though I hated Declan, I couldn't sit by while a group of stupid girls made fun of him. It was obvious he'd been trying to hide his scar until now.

I fucked up more than I did right at practice. My head wasn't in the right place. All I kept thinking about was how hurt he looked and then shut it away. I was sure that when he took this coaching job, Declan never thought they'd make fun of him.

Once practice was over, I didn't even shower. I grabbed my bag and headed for the boys. I needed to be grounded. My mind was all over the place, and I was afraid I'd slip. I wanted to hit the track and run for hours and only stop once my body gave out. I knew Oz would ground me. He would instantly know something was wrong with me and try to make it better.

I wasn't wrong. I'd barely stepped into the stadium where they could see me, and Oz's head was directed my way. I didn't try to hide what I was feeling. It wouldn't do me any good. Oz jogged over to his coach and talked to him for only a second before he left the field and met me at the bottom of the bleachers.

One minute my mind was swirling with darkness and the next I was calm. Oz's arms wrapped around me, and he pulled me into a hug so tight it felt as if he'd never let me go.

After what felt like an hour and only a second at the same time, Oz kissed the top of my head and muttered. "Everything's going to be alright."

Pulling away, I looked up at my twin. God, how I'd missed him while we lived apart. It was then I decided wherever his life with Lo took him, I was going to follow. Why not? They were two of the best people I knew. "How can you be so sure?"

"Because you came to me and didn't hide. That's the

first step." He tugged on the end of my ponytail. "Do you want to tell me what happened?"

"Not really," I murmured as I pulled out of his hold. I could feel the eyes of the entire team on me, but I didn't care. All I cared about was that my insides didn't feel like they were equal parts ready to explode and crawling to be free from my body. "Go finish practice and once you're done, I might be ready to tell you."

I knew I wouldn't be, but I would tell him. I just didn't want to break down in front of his entire team.

Instead of watching their practice, I laid on the bleachers and let the sun burn away all my overly complicated thoughts. It didn't work, but it did boost my already golden skin to another level. All of our practices were giving me a healthy glow that had been absent for the last year of my life even with all the sunscreen I applied. Last year it didn't seem to matter how much time I spent in the sun, my skin was always pasty white. Maybe that had to do with how sick my body was. I didn't know, but I liked having a tan, so I didn't have to wear makeup.

I must have fallen asleep because one second, I was thinking about how tan I was getting and how school would be starting soon and the next I was in the shade with my twin hovering over me and his friends sitting around me.

Crunching up to sit, I swung my legs to the side and looked at everyone around me. "What's going on?"

"Nothing," Ford shrugged one shoulder. "We were waiting on you to wake up."

Inwardly I cringed. How long had they been waiting?

"Well, I'm up now. Are you ready to go home?" Without waiting for them to answer, I grabbed my bag and started down the bleachers.

A warm arm around came around my shoulders and I sunk into Oz's embrace. I wanted to kick myself all over again for not following him here in the first place. I thought I was going to be someone special, but in the end, I turned into a nobody and almost lost myself along the way. None of that would have happened if I was here. With our bond, Oz would have known something was wrong and intervened. It wasn't like he hadn't known something was happening to me, but being apart let me push his concerns away. Plus, with all that was happening with Lo, he was preoccupied.

Ford came up on my other side and grinned at me. He was so damn hot. If he hadn't found his person in his professor last year, I probably would have hit on my brother's friend. I definitely had a type. Strong, tall, dark, and handsome. All things that Declan was in spades. "I'm going to come over and make dinner tonight."

"Oh, yeah?" All thoughts of Declan instantly

forgotten. "What are you going to make?" I tried to hide how unenthusiastic I was at the possibility of what he might make. I knew Ford came over way more often than he needed to just to feed me. He'd been busy all summer with his new boyfriend, trying to do fun things that couples should do before school started and they had to hide they were a couple. Yet he still came over multiple times a week and when he knew he'd be busy he had meals in containers ready for me. And the guys, too, but he always made me and Lo something different from them. I should be eating what the guys ate, but I'd needed to pack on the pounds before the season started. I still wasn't where I should be, but that wasn't Ford's fault. It was all mine.

"Steak, mashed potatoes, and asparagus with corn bread," he called as he broke away and headed toward his car.

Tears formed in my eyes. Ford was making me my favorite comfort meal. Damn these guys were too good to me.

I slipped into the backseat and waited for someone to ask me what had happened earlier, but the car was strangely quiet. At least until Fin spoke up.

"We could burn his house down."

West shot daggers at Fin while Oz shook his head and chuckled. "That is not an option. Ever." West turned to look at me. "Don't listen to him. Sometimes he gets these little pyromaniac tendencies, but do not take him up on his offer under any circumstances."

I had thought both West and Fin were kidding, but after that, I wasn't so sure.

"No houses need to be burned down. I'm mad at myself not *him*."

"What happened?"

"I got soft when I shouldn't have, but those bitches…" I curled my hands into fists at my sides and then told them everything as we headed home. Even once we parked in the driveway, they listened to every word I had to say before we all piled out and headed inside.

"I still say we burn his house down," Fin said as he flopped down on the couch.

West shot daggers at him and then turned his attention back to me. "As you can see, he's not the best at vengeance."

"And you are?" Fin laughed. "Dani, you do what you can do. What feels right to you. But maybe you've changed your mind after today."

I dropped my bag by the door and headed into the kitchen for some water. "Just because I have a soft spot because he's physically hurt doesn't mean I still don't want him to go down." How was I going to pin him sleeping with a player if they were all bitches and making fun of him? Maybe that was why I was pissed. They'd ruined my plan. But I knew that wasn't the case. I felt for Declan even though I didn't want to.

"I'm going to go to my room and try to take a nap." I told the room. Lo was still asleep otherwise I would have talked to her. Not that she'd have a plan to help me out, but she'd understand why I was having these rioting emotions. But instead of sleeping, I laid down and went over every girl on the team and tried to think if I'd seen any of them look at Declan like they wanted him. Most of them had because he was hot as fuck. The bad thing was I didn't know any of them. Hell, I didn't even have a single one's phone number. Maybe I could break into someone's locker, take their phone, and start texting him with it.

I was desperate that was plain and simple. Plus, I wasn't usually devious. I didn't have an inner mean girl unless it came to my ex. I guess I'd just have to improvise. You know what they say. Fake it until you make it.

FIVE

DECLAN

AFTER YESTERDAY it was a wonder how I pulled myself out of bed today, but somehow, I managed it. It was strange to miss living with my sister, Roxie. I hadn't wanted to move in and recover at her house, but I had. It was the best decision I'd ever made. It had only brought us closer. Now it was strange to walk through a quiet house and not hear her shuffling through papers, or humming to herself while she was in the kitchen.

Why had I taken the job as assistant coach here? Oh yeah, to make my sister stop worrying about me. I saw how much she wanted me to get off the couch and do something besides stew in my anger that my soccer career was over. I never thought Danica would show up, nor did I think I would be coaching a team full of college age women.

I dreaded each limped step I took onto the field. I faced forward while my eyes roamed for the one person I wanted to see, but she was nowhere to be found. Was she going to skip practice after what happened yesterday? I wouldn't blame her. I wanted to do the same thing. My leg still burned with constant pain. I couldn't have anything touch my scar. It was oversensitive after having a cleat dug into it.

"Alright, you've done enough stretching. I want everyone up to run the three-mile route. I'll be timing you and if your time isn't to my liking, you'll run an extra three once regular practice is over." I blew my whistle and then hit my stopwatch.

All of the girls jumped up and glared at me as they took off. Just as the last one was out of view, Dani jogged onto the field and looked around.

"Did you cancel practice because I wasn't here?" she laughed bitterly.

"Not on your life, sweetheart. They're running, and you should join them. Now," I growled. I knew I shouldn't be taking my anger out on Dani when none of this was her fault, but I couldn't help it. I was falling back into old patterns.

"I will," she spat as she took off lightning fast. I knew she'd catch up and would likely be the first one back. She was that good. Again, I wanted to ask her why she ended up here. I knew logically it was because her brother lived here, but what made her give up on UCLA? I'd probably never know.

Slowly I moved to where the girls would be coming back in and waited for them to arrive. Coach Parker wasn't here again today. I wasn't sure what was going on with her, but I was starting to wonder if they brought me on to replace her. She was at the doctor's office more often than at practice these days. I hadn't asked any questions since we weren't friends. We were barely work associates. If she wanted to tell me she would.

Like I thought, Dani was the first to run by me, her eyes narrowed, and she was barely out of breath. I watched the way her ass moved in her shorts and the bounce of her tits in her sports bra. She was too thin but beautiful, even without makeup and dressed in her workout gear.

She jogged around the field once, sat down only a few feet away from me, and started to stretch. "Where's Coach Parker?"

"The doctor," I answered back with a bite while looking off in the distance for the next person to arrive.

"Is this how you're going to treat me after yesterday? Hell, even after the other day when I made sure you were okay and I got you ice?" she snapped.

Turning to face her, I found Dani bent over with her

chest to her legs. Damn, I forgot how limber she was. "I didn't ask for any of that."

"No, I guess you didn't. I guess I should have left you in the middle of the field, so you could crawl to the bench to get your phone." She shrugged and stretched to her left facing away from me. "Next time, if there is a next time, I'll leave you to rot like you did me."

"What the hell are you talking about?" I shouted. I hadn't meant to especially with a group of five girls headed straight for me.

"It doesn't matter. I'm done with you. Don't even talk to me unless it's absolutely necessary. Do you hear me?" She turned her head to look my way, and I saw an avalanche of hurt in her eyes.

"Yeah, I hear you."

I wasn't sure I'd ever be able to make things right between us. The only time she talked to me was when I was hurt, but I wasn't willing for that to happen again.

I called out times as the girls came in. They were already getting faster, but they needed to be more of *everything* to win. I wasn't used to losing, and when I took this job, I had no idea how bad the team had been in previous years. If it had been up to me, I would have had all new try outs, but it wasn't. Maybe next year.

"Split up in groups of four," I ordered. They all moaned but did as directed. Except for Dani. She stood by herself staring at the goal to her left as if she didn't hear me. "Francisco, get with a team."

Her gaze whipped my way, and if she could have murdered me with her eyes, Danica would have done it. She'd only taken one step and I saw the rest of the girls tense. No one wanted her with them. This wasn't going to work. They needed to think like a team. Not like Dani was the enemy.

It didn't help that I didn't know most of their names. I was learning but slowly. Names weren't really in my wheelhouse which I told the athletic department *before* they hired me.

"Goalies, take a goal," I barked out. I was going to whip them into shape and into a team if it was the last thing I did. "Alright, ladies since you don't want to be a team today, we're going to let your feet decide for you who you'll be paired up with.

"What?" Was the collective reaction from most of the girls.

"Don't question me. Now line up."

A moan resounded around the field, but I didn't care. I would make their lives miserable if they were going to act like spoiled children. Dani included.

"Line up by your numbers. If you don't get the ball in, I want you to move to the left side of the field, and if you make it, move to the right."

Technically they all should be able to make it in. If not, why were they on the team?

Out of the thirty girls, eight didn't make their shot. I was getting ready to order them to practice making goals when Coach Parker stepped up beside me.

"Can I talk to you?" Her voice was quiet. Solemn.

Did they know about my previous relationship with Danica? Was this the end of me coaching here?

"Yeah, sure. Give me a moment to get the girls onto their next drill." Less than two minutes later, I was on the side of the field with my hands clasped behind my back waiting for her to tell me whatever she came out here to say. When she called early this morning to tell me I'd be in charge, I didn't think she'd show up. "Is everything okay?"

"It depends on how you look at it. I'm going to need to step back from a majority of my duties here, which means we'll need you to step in or find someone else who is willing to."

"What's going on?"

Maybe this was what I needed to get away from Danica. If I didn't have to see her five days a week, I could finish mourning the end of our relationship.

"I have cancer," she croaked out and blinked back tears. "I have surgery next week, and then start treatment quickly afterward. The prognosis looks... decent, but we're going at it aggressively. My doctors have informed me, I'm going to likely be weak and sick. I don't want to be here once or twice a week to step in on what you're doing the rest of the days. It would be easier if you took over. If you're willing."

Looking out at the field, my eyes searched out Dani. The second my gaze landed on her it was as if she could feel me looking. She looked up from where she stood and met my own before she went back to her footwork.

"If it's too much I'll understand. I know there was an incident the other day when I was gone."

"It was nothing." Parker gave me a dubious look. "It aggravated an old injury that's all."

"I'll understand if you don't want to do it. You didn't sign up for this much work, and I know you've never been a coach before."

Did she doubt I could do it?

"But you were a talented player and any knowledge and skills you can bring to the table could help these girls tremendously."

"So, I'd have full say?" I was already picking off girls in my head at the thought.

"You'd technically be head coach. Whatever you do or say goes."

"What if I want to hold try outs?"

Coach Parker hung her head. "I know these girls

aren't the best, and unfortunately we haven't ranked high over the years, so we're not sought-after like some schools, but we do the best we can with what we've got."

She wasn't saying no.

"It's still early, and I'd like to…"

Parker placed her hand on my shoulder lightly and looked up at me. Her brown doe eyes looking up at me with pity. "We're not going to have a stack of girls like Danica. Let's face it plain and simple." She shook her head. "I was actually quite shocked when she called me up and asked if she could be on the team." She laughed, looking out at Dani. "I certainly wasn't going to say no. I know she's going to regret her decision to come here, I'm hoping with both of your skills it will encourage the others to want to do better."

"Danica's brother goes to school here. It's probably why she's here."

"Oh, I forget you two might know each other. Did you ever meet when you were both attending UCLA?"

"Yeah, we knew each other." I definitely wasn't going to divulge our history. If the school knew we'd once had a relationship together they'd likely fire me instead of trying to promote me when I was only two weeks into a job, I'd never done before.

"But why switch now?" She asked quietly as if Dani

would be able to hear her from across the field and over all the noise.

"No, idea. But I sure as hell wish I knew."

"I know this is a lot to ask of you, but I really think you'll do an amazing job. If you need any guidance, I'll only be a phone call away."

I couldn't fathom calling her knowing the reason she wasn't here was because she was sick at home.

"Are you going to come in at all, or are you fully stepping back?"

"It depends on what you want. I want to make this as easy for you as possible. We can hire someone to be the assistant coach to help you." She sighed and looked off in the distance. "I should have had this conversation with you and the athletic board, but I didn't want it to be impersonal. I don't have all the specifics. I knew this might be a possibility, and I've thought long and hard about what's best for these girls and I think that's you. It's up to you whether you want to take on that challenge."

It was like she knew exactly what to say to get to me. There was no way in hell I wouldn't rise up and transform these girls into the best players they could possibly be.

Turning to look out at my team a grin slowly grew on my face. "Does this mean I get a raise?"

Parker clapped me on the shoulder. "And my office."

Damn I kind of felt bad about that, but I knew she

was doing what was best for her and that was stepping back and getting healthy.

"You've got yourself a head coach then." I laughed. It was strange how not even six months ago, I could barely get out of bed thinking my life was over. This might not have been where I saw my life going when I was in Spain, but it wasn't turning out too bad. Willow Bay wanted me for my talent just not in the way I thought I'd use it, and my sister and I were closer than ever. The unexpected gift was I had Danica back in my life.

And she was going to hate me even more when she learned I was the head coach.

I couldn't wait to see her face and the wrath that would surely come with it.

SIX

DANICA

"I KNOW this is coming out of nowhere for some of you, and I wouldn't leave if there was any other option, but I have to step away for this season."

My only season here.

"But," Coach Parker gave us a wobbly smile before she continued. "Coach Hart will be taking over. With him, you're going to go far this season, I just know it."

There were a couple of hoots and hollers, but all I could do was stare at Declan and wonder if he was going to let this go to his head. I wasn't sure I could take him bossing me around at practice and games all of the time.

"I've already seen great improvement from the majority of you since Coach Hart has been with us, and I want that to continue. While this may be his first-year coaching, he… he knows what he's doing. With that said and our first preseason game coming soon, there will be try outs for the team."

"What?" Half the team shouted.

It was probably the half that shouldn't have been on the team to begin with.

"It's going to be open to anyone who wants to try out, and Coach Hart will be deciding who will be on the team this year." She bit down on her bottom lip and scanned over us. "I'll be here as often as I can, but that won't be much, and I'm sorry. I wish things were different."

She shouldn't be apologizing for taking care of herself. I know this better than most here. That's *why* I was here. I knew I wasn't going to be on the best team when I decided to transfer here, but I knew with one hundred perfect certainty it was the best decision for me. That was until I saw Declan, now I wasn't too sure. If Oz wasn't here to keep me on the right path, I would have spiraled already. Hell, I was already slipping, and I didn't even want to.

I would do better. For myself and those that loved me.

"We're going to have practice like normal, but on Friday there will be try outs. I have put out the word all over. Do I think we'll get hundreds from around the country? No, but I want this team to have the opportunity to be the best that it can be. So, this Friday, I want you all to give it everything you've got. If not, you might not get a number."

My gaze drifted to Declan. It was the first time I'd look at him since they called this meeting. Luckily, he wasn't looking at me. Once my eyes were on him, I couldn't help but take him in. The attraction was still there. It had never stopped, and that pissed me off. How could my traitorous body still want him after he broke my heart? Broke me?

Declan was tall and lean like most soccer players. His bronzed skin glowed in the sunlight. But it was his eyes that had the twinkle back that had been lacking every day on the field.

Except when he was talking to you.

That didn't matter though. What mattered was if he was going to take advantage of his new position. I wasn't sure how much more of him I could take, and I didn't want him to break me.

Turning with his hands on his hips, Declan locked eyes with me. "If you're not here on Friday for try outs, we will take that to mean that you no longer want to be on the team."

Was this his way of giving me an out?

I guess I had a few days to decide if I wanted to play under him or not.

"I know you've been hit with a shock today, so we're going to keep this easy. Run the three mile circuit, and get yourself centered. Talk. Do whatever you have to do. When you get back, we'll run some drills, and then the day will be over." He clapped his hands and then blew his whistle. "Go."

I jumped to my feet and headed out. I couldn't wait to pound the pavement. The others were following. I barely heard them since they were all talking and falling behind.

While I had questions, there was only one person who could answer them, and that was one person I was unwilling to talk to. At least right now. I needed time to process and maybe talk to my therapist and my family.

Lo sat down on the couch beside me, and Charlie jumped up next to her. "Is everything okay?"

Leaning my head on her shoulder, I blew out a breath. "I don't know. I'm trying to figure out if I should stay on the team or not."

Her shoulder jerked and then one of Lo's hands was smoothing down my hair. "Talk to me. I'm still your best friend, right?"

I sat up with my jaw hanging open. "Of course, you

are. I love you, Lo, and I'm sorry I haven't been talking to you about everything that's going on with me, but…"

"You wanted to make sure I was healed…" she grimaced.

"You are healed," I whispered as if it was too loud it wouldn't be true.

"With the way everyone still keeps tiptoeing around me as if I'll break, you wouldn't think so." Lo pouted.

"They do the same with me. Maybe we need to have a meeting and tell them to stop babying us."

"Except Ford cooking for us. I'm not sure I'm ready to give that up. After this year, we'll have to cook for ourselves. Oz isn't going to be impressed with my shitty cooking, and I doubt I can convince Ford and Xander to let us move in with them." She giggled.

"Doubtful. Since I'll most likely be single for the rest of my life, I'll move in with you and cook. I might not be as awesome as Ford, but at least I don't burn water."

"Hey." She swatted me.

"It's true."

"All but you being single forever. Is that what's bothering you?"

"Being single is the least of my worries. According to my therapist, I'm not even supposed to be in a relationship. Not that I want one. I'm not ready." If I got hurt again, I wasn't sure I'd recover.

"Well, you're a catch, so once you're ready you'll find the right guy. Just have fun while you're in college."

A bitter laugh slipped out. "I doubt this year will be much fun. I either stop playing the sport I love, or have Declan lording over me all the time."

Lo turned to face me. Her blue eyes narrowed. I knew it wasn't at me, but the situation. "What are you talking about? Has he been giving you problems?"

"I don't know. Today at practice we were told he's going to be the head coach from now on, and there's tryouts on Friday."

A loud knock on the front door kept me from saying more.

"What the hell?" Lo jumped up. "Are you expecting anyone?"

I stood and stared at the door with her. "You're my only friend here, so no."

Another loud knock had Fin storming down the hallway like he was going to murder whoever was at the door. I wouldn't put it past him.

"What the hell are you doing here?" Fin growled, blocking the door.

"I came to see Dani. Is she here?" A familiar voice drifted from the front door.

"Is that Declan?" Lo whispered at my side.

I nodded and started to take a step back until Lo gripped my arm and steadied me.

"You should talk to him."

Not what I expected my friend for almost a decade to say. Whose side was she on?

"What if I don't want to hear what he has to say?" Even as I said those words, I took a step forward.

Lo didn't answer. I was halfway to the door when I looked back over my shoulder, and she gave me an encouraging smile.

Placing my hand on his forearm, I tried my best to sound confident. "Thanks Fin, but I've got this."

It didn't escape my notice Declan's eyes were trained on where I was touching Fin, or the tick in his jaw. Did he seriously not remember that Fin was gay and with West? I wanted to roll my eyes at him, but instead I closed the front door behind me, and sat down on the bottom step of the porch. Everyone could probably still hear us, but I wanted to make it as difficult as possible.

After several long seconds of silence, I looked over my shoulder to find Declan staring at me in the exact same spot he was when I walked outside. I wasn't going to be weak for him. No longer. "Say what you came to say. I'm busy."

"I know I probably shouldn't have come here—"

"You think?" I interrupted him.

Declan moved off the porch and stood in front of me. "I didn't know where else to find you."

"I'm either here or at practice. Where else did you expect to find me?"

He swallowed harshly. I swore I could see his Adam's apple get stuck in the middle for a moment. "You live here."

I wasn't sure if it was a question or a statement. Either way, I answered him. "Yes, I live here with my brother and his friends. Do you have a problem with that?"

"Not at all," he said while he nodded. I wasn't sure if he knew he was giving me mixed messages, but I didn't care. The only thing I wanted to know was why Declan was here in the first place. Was he going to tell me not to try out on Friday?

"Why are you here, Coach?" I ground out the last word.

He flinched but kept his face on lock down. I hated it when he hid what he was thinking, but I guess I didn't really have any right to ask for more. Not now.

His hands clenched into fists at his side. "Listen, I didn't ask to be made head coach, and I had to think long and hard on whether I would take the position now that you're here."

I hopped up. My hands resting on my hips. "So, if I

wasn't in the picture, it would have been an easy decision for you to make?"

"Easier." He looked down at his sneakers for a long moment and when he looked up, my Declan was standing before me. The one who showed me what he was feeling. His chocolaty orbs radiated sadness. "I know you hate me, and I don't blame you. I didn't handle my injury well, and I completely cut you out of my life. That's all on me." He swallowed roughly again. "I don't know why you're here, Dani, and not at UCLA, but I want to help you as much as possible if you'll let me."

"I don't need your help. The reason I'm on the team is because I love the sport. Not because I planned on winning or thought we'd make the championship." Unable to look at him when I said what I needed to say next, I shifted toward the street. "I know my chances at the Olympics are gone."

His hand raised and then lowered back at his side. Declan's voice was so quiet I barely heard him as he asked. "What happened Dani?"

"It's none of your business. We aren't together anymore."

"Maybe not, but I'm still your coach."

"Yeah, unfortunately you are, but that doesn't mean I'm going to tell you." Crossing my arms over my chest, I looked to him. "Is that all you came to say?"

"Fuck," he shouted, clutching his head in his hands.

For one brief second, I wanted to reach out and touch him. That was until I remembered how he ghosted me and then he magically showed up as my soccer coach.

"Stay on the team even if I'm the coach." He raked his fingers through his hair before lifting his face. His tortured eyes met mine. "But only if you want to. When I took this job months ago, I had no idea you'd be on the team."

"And if you knew, would you have declined?"

"I don't think you want to know the answer to that." He took two steps and then turned back. "Will I see you at try outs?"

I didn't think I was the best of the best, but I knew hands down I was the best on the Blackhawks women's team. The fact that I had to try out when all I'd done was make a call before was ludicrous, but whatever.

"You'll either see me or you won't." I shrugged. "But either way, don't come back here. I'm not sure I'll be able to stop the next person who wants to kick your ass."

His eyes trailed over me and then to the house before coming back to me. "For what it's worth, I'm sorry, Dani. I wish I had handled the situation a whole hell of a lot differently, but I can't change the past."

"And neither can I." I waved. "I'll see you when I see you."

One hundred and ninety percent, I was going to be at try outs. Even on my worst day, I out played all the girls here. I would make the team, but Declan didn't need to know that. I wanted him to sweat wondering if I'd show up or not. He was in serious denial if he thought he was magically going to turn this team towards a championship win. At least not unless he replaced ninety-nine percent of the team.

I didn't look back as I walked up the stairs and went inside. Declan Hart would never again have a hold on my heart or my decisions.

DANICA

"OF COURSE, THAT BITCH MADE IT," someone whispered angrily. I'm not sure how they thought I wasn't going to make the team, but whatever. Since I only knew a few of their names, I didn't give a shit if they did or didn't make the team.

Declan had surprisingly delivered. Ten girls from across the U.S. showed up on Friday to tryout, and I couldn't say that I was mad about it. With them on the team, we might actually have a chance at a decent season.

"Take it in girls, because tomorrow I want you on the field and giving me a hundred and ten percent," Declan barked out from his office door.

"God, he's an asshole."

"But a hot asshole."

"I know, right?"

"Wouldn't you be an asshole if your career was over, and you had that hideous scar that he tried to hide in the beginning?"

A group of girls whispered loudly next to me.

I rolled my eyes not even trying to hide how ridiculous I thought they were. It took everything I had in me to bite my tongue and not go off on them, but I didn't need the attention of sticking up for him. Nor did I want Declan to think I gave a shit about him.

I watched one of the new girls, who I thought was named Sabrina and had made the team, sidled up to Declan. She pushed her ample chest out as she fluttered her eyelashes at him. She was beautiful in a way that I wasn't. She had long, black hair that cascaded down her back. Her olive skin was flawless, and her body was muscular and toned. She was perfect and I hated her in that moment.

Sabrina giggled and casually but not casually placed her hand on his arm. It clicked right then and there. I smiled, turned on my heel and headed out of the building. I had a little skip in my step as I made my way over to the football field. The boys practice was still going on as I made my way up the bleachers and sat down to wait for them.

If I wanted to, I could have run home, but now that a plan was forming in my head, I was the happiest I'd been in a long time. Definitely happier than any moment in the last year.

Oz turned and looked up at me with a worried expression on his face. Did he really think I wouldn't make the team? I barely even broke a sweat. I gave him a big smile and a wave. It wasn't until I saw his shoulders drop that I noticed he was tense.

Even though I doubted he'd be able to read my lips, I mouthed 'I'm good.' I hated that I was causing stress in his life when he was finally happy.

Placing my hands behind me, I leaned back and tilted my face up to the sun. Letting the rays warm me from the outside in, I formulated a plan to ruin Declan. It didn't matter that Coach Parker was out for the season. As far as I was concerned, the team could go down as long as Declan got what was coming for him.

"What's got you smiling?" West said, startling me.

"Jesus, West," I gasped with my hand to my chest. "You nearly gave me a heart attack."

"Sorry," he smiled telling me he wasn't sorry as he sat down beside me. "I guess you made the team."

"Did you guys really doubt I would make it?"

He shrugged. "I don't doubt your ability, but I thought maybe your ex might make it difficult for you."

I couldn't help but scoff. "If he wants to win and keep his job, he better keep me."

West chuckled beside me and looked out at the field. "Are you regretting coming here?"

"Probably not for the reason you think I am." West was slated to be drafted in the NFL this coming Spring, and he knew my chances at my dream were slim to none now. I was still smiling though.

"I'm not going to assume why you regret it, but I would like to know, so maybe I can help."

West really was sweet. I wasn't sure how he ended up with an asshole like Fin. The only thing I did know was that West was the best thing to ever happen to Fin. Fin was a much better human once he met the love of his life. I guess everyone was if they got to keep them. Not that Declan was the love of my life. I was sure eventually I'd find my person.

"This time in Oz and Lo's lives should be happy one, and they spend all their time worrying about me. I hate it." Curling my hands around my too thin thighs, I stared down at my all-black tennis shoes. "If I would have gone home with my parents everyone here could live their lives."

"Your brother and Lo would be heartbroken if they heard you say that. They both love you so much, and while they do worry about you. We all do," West amended. "We want you here in Willow Bay. No one knows where we'll all be headed once we graduate, and we want to spend it with the ones that matter to us."

I wanted to say if we all mean so much to each other wouldn't we all be in each other's lives after college, but I knew West was stressed about if he'd be drafted and where he'd be sent. He had no control over where his future took him.

"I don't even know what I'm going to do after this year," I admitted.

"Most people don't. Not unless they've already got something lined up, but I know you're going to do great. You're so smart and your determination to work past any obstacles is admirable."

"Thanks," I mumbled while cringing on the inside. While everyone would be off living their lives, I still had two years of school left to become a physical therapist once I graduated.

"I'm sure Fin would let you stay in the house if you wanted to continue going to school here."

A burst of laughter flew from my mouth before I could contain it. "Yeah, right. Not unless you asked him and performed sexual favors."

"It would be no hardship for me to ask for you," he winked at me.

"Well, I might just take you up on your offer since I have no idea where I'll go next."

"Maybe talk to your brother." He nudged his shoulder into mine. "Let him know how you're feeling. He might surprise you."

"He won't because he's always supportive." Looking into his light green eyes, I swallowed down the emotion that was threatening to take over. "I wish I could be normal again."

"Normal is overrated," Fin said as he took a stance in front of us. He was a sneaky bastard. I wasn't sure how I missed his arrival. "Embrace who you are, and you'll be much happier."

West stood and brushed his hand against Fin's. They didn't show much outward affection toward each other when they were outside of the house. It wasn't as if the entire team didn't know they were together, but it was best not to remind them. It didn't help that a fraternity assaulted West their freshmen year because he was gay.

"You're right." I jumped up. "I'd hug you if I didn't think you'd cringe."

Fin's entire body stiffened. His face went blank. Which in turn made me laugh.

"But I won't. Don't worry. Let's get out of here, I need your help."

"Mine?" Fin gestured to himself.

"Yeah, I need your devious brain to help me come up

with a plan. I've already started formulating it, but I want to make sure it's perfect."

"You're hitting my heartstrings. I might just hug *you*," Fin said in the most sarcastic, but loving in his own way tone.

"Now you're just messing with me. But seriously, thank you. Both of you."

"For what?" West asked as he rounded the car and opened the passenger door.

"For being here for me. It means a lot that you let me into your house. You could have sent me off to live in the dorms or an apartment by myself."

"You should be thanking Ford for moving in with Xander, not us." Fin deadpanned as if he had done nothing for me.

"Thank you anyway." I seriously would have hugged him if I didn't know how uncomfortable it would make him. "Where's Oz?" I thought he would have been the first one out instead of the last.

"He was talking to Coach when I came out. Said to give him a few," Fin answered. He must have been in a good mood because this was the most he had spoken to me in a long time.

Oz bounded out of the building and straight to the car with an easy smile on his face. He slid into the backseat with me and put his arm around my shoulders.

"What's got you so chipper?" Fin asked as he started the car and drove out of the parking lot.

"Is it not enough that our weekend is here, and Ford is coming by to cook for us?"

"Are you really that happy that this is our last one-day practice until the season starts?" Fin grumbled.

"You know if it wasn't so fucking hot, they could just keep us practicing all day. Now would you rather have that or come back when the sun isn't beating down on us?"

With no time like the present, I decided now would be a perfect time to bring up what West and I talked about. "What do you think you're going to do once you graduate?"

"Marry Lo," he answered simply.

Turning, I hugged my brother and smiled into his shoulder. I desperately wanted what he and Lo had. They were so certain in their love for each other. "After that, where do you see yourself working or living?"

"He's moving wherever we go," Fin answered for my twin.

"I'll probably stay here in California. Probably move closer to LA. I don't know. Where do you see yourself?"

"That's the thing. I have no idea. I have two more years of school to become a physical therapist, and I'm not sure where to do it."

Resting his cheek on top of my head, he spoke quietly. "Where do you want to finish?"

"That I don't know either. Maybe I'll follow you."

"Sounds like everyone is following us then," Fin joked.

"Doubtful since I probably won't be in California, but you're all welcome to follow us. Although I can't say how long we'll be wherever we go."

Fin and Oz both scoffed, but it was Fin who spoke. "There's no way whoever gets you won't keep you. You're too talented. Once they get you, they won't let go."

"Aw," I cooed from the backseat. "That's seriously sweet."

"It's the truth," Fin argued like just because it was the truth it couldn't be sweet. He pulled into our driveway and put the car in park. Turning around he leveled his black eyes on me. "Now do we want these two helping us come up with a plan or should we keep it to just the two of us."

"What plan?" Oz asked, shouldering his bag.

"To take down her ex," Fin answered simply.

Oz's blond brows furrowed. "Wait. I thought you made the team. You came into practice beaming. Did that asshole jilt you again?" He growled out.

At least Oz expected me to make the team, but I still rolled my eyes. "I'm on the team and we might actually be halfway decent with the new people he brought on. I still want to take him down."

"Will it really make you happy to see him fired?" He grabbed my bag and started to head for the house. "At least that's what I assume you're trying for."

"It wouldn't hurt."

Fin clapped my brother on the back. "Let your sister have her revenge. It will make her feel better. This is the happiest I've seen her since she got here. It's like having the old Dani back."

"You're seriously trying hard for a hug today." I held my arms open and took a step toward Fin as he took a step back.

"I'm not going to help you if you're going to keep trying for a hug. I get that I'm hot and have an amazing body, but it's not for you."

It was almost impossible to fight back my smile.

"While it's true, I can't believe you just said that." West shook his head and chuckled. "Come on Oz. Let's leave these two to plan."

"What?" My brother almost shouted. "How are you on board with this?"

West widened his stance in front of Fin and crossed his arms over his chest. "Because first I'm going to lay down a simple ground rule. Don't do anything that could possibly get you arrested or expelled."

"I'm just helping plan, but sure." Fin shrugged like it was no big deal. "We won't burn down his house or anything. It will be simple vengeance."

"As if there is such a thing," Oz mumbled as he strode up the steps to the front door. He turned to look at me before going inside where I was sure he was going to have sex with my best friend. "Just be careful."

"Always, brother."

We waited for them to be inside. The second the front door closed; Fin turned to me. "What do you have in mind?"

"I know I turned down your idea before, but with the new girls that were added to the team, I saw serious potential. I just need your help on how to go about framing them."

"You've come to the right place. Let's take that asshole down."

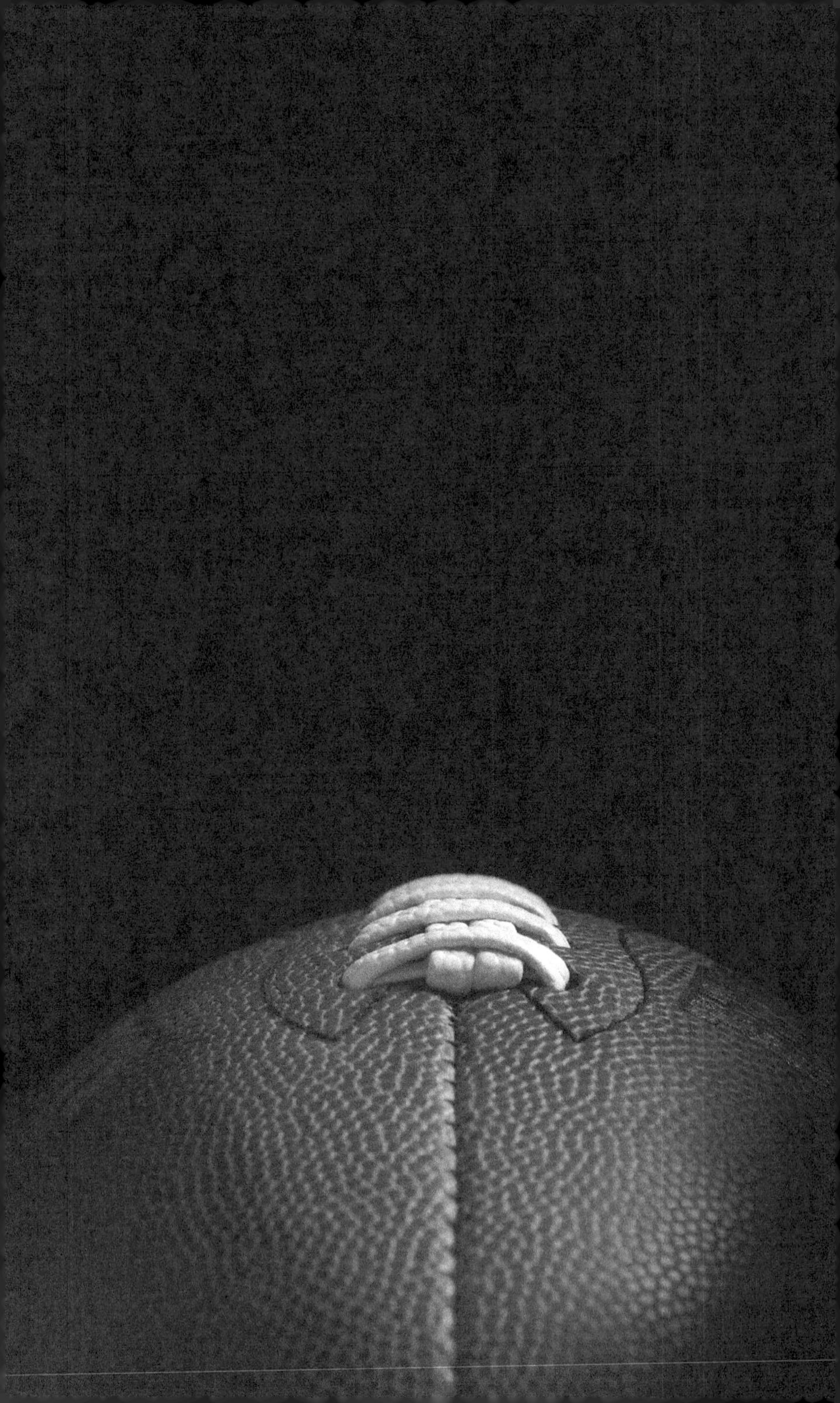

EIGHT

DECLAN

1 Month Later

MY BLOOD WAS NEARLY BOILING as I made my way down the hall of the hotel, straight to Danica's room. She'd gone too far.

"That fucking bitch," I growled, startling a couple as I passed them. "Sorry," I muttered in apology. It wasn't their fault I was nearly exploding out in the hallway.

Rounding on Dani's room, I slammed my fist into her door as I banged on it. I didn't care if almost everyone else in the hotel was asleep. This was not going to wait.

I kept banging until her door swung open and a stunned Danica stood in front of me in only a t-shirt.

"What the hell, Declan?" She squinted up at me. Her long blonde hair was a mess letting me know she had indeed been in bed when I arrived. The thought of her warm, soft skin from sleeping nearly had me forgetting what I was here for.

"You've gone too fucking far," I gritted out as I pushed my way into her room.

Closing the hotel room's door, she leaned up against it. Her face was one of innocence. Fake innocence. "And what is it I've supposedly done?"

"Do you want to explain to me why I found Katie in my room? In my bed?" I shouted, "And not even a few moments later a group of four girls from the team at my door?"

"I have no idea what you're talking about. What you have with Katie is your business. Not mine." She cocked her head to the side and I instantly knew she was lying. It was her tell.

"Stop fucking lying," I barked out, and stepped toward her. "Are you trying to get me fired?"

"As a matter of fact, I am. Have I succeeded yet?" she smiled sweetly.

"What the fuck is wrong with you?"

"You," she shouted, pushing off the door and invading my space.

"Don't fuck with me little girl. You won't like the consequences."

Dani let out a maniacal laugh. "I'm not sure there's much worse I could go through, but you sure as hell can try."

"What is that supposed to mean?"

"Like I'm going to tell you." She poked me in the chest.

I stood staring at the woman I used to know, wondering where she went. How had she changed so much? The Danica I knew was light and happy. Now she was bitter and full of rage.

"Why don't you go back to your orgy and let me get back to my sleep? Someone's gotta try and win the game for us tomorrow." She pressed into me. Her full, perky breasts brushed my chest.

And I snapped.

Gripping her by the hair, I yanked her head back as I slammed my mouth into hers. Dani's body went ridged before she tried to push me away. If there was one person on this goddamn team I was going to be fucking tonight, it was going to be her.

With my free hand, I wrenched her leg up and wrapped it around my waist before I slid my hand up her inner thigh only to find Danica wasn't wearing anything underneath her t-shirt. Plunging my tongue into her mouth as I thrust two fingers deep inside her tight heat, I nearly came on the spot when her walls clenched around me.

Even as her hands pressed against me to get out of my hold, her hips bucked into my hand, and her tongue danced with mine. She shuddered in my arms, and I knew I had my Dani back.

Pain lanced through my tongue causing me to pull back from our kiss.

"What the hell do you think you're doing?" She said breathlessly even as she had her eyes narrowed.

"Showing you that you're the only person I want to sleep with on this team."

"Oh, I'm so lucky," she scoffed and then moaned as I curled my fingers deep inside of her.

"I certainly think so, and maybe after I ply an orgasm out of you, you'll tell me what the hell is wrong with you."

Her body stiffened and not in the good way. With more force than I thought she was capable of, Dani shoved me off her. She scurried over to the bed, curled on her side, and pulled the blanket up to her chin.

"Dani," I huffed as I crawled onto the bed and hovered over her. Pushing her onto her back, I ripped the blanket to the side. My hand found familiar territory as it skated up her leg and under the t-shirt. Dani had the softest skin I'd ever felt in my life, and I knew those tits of hers were even better.

"Stop," she whispered. A crack in that one word.

My hand halted and when my eyes went to hers, they were glassy and her chin was trembling.

"Dani," my voice broke as my heart constricted in my chest. My entire body started to shake. "I would never hurt you."

"You already have," she croaked out.

"How? Tell me what I did," I demanded softly.

She shook her head franticly. "How can you not know? One day you're talking to me and the next you cut me off. When I tried to call you again, you'd blocked me. Why you care now when you didn't then, I don't know? But it's too little, too late."

My body went ramrod straight from her words. "I wasn't in a good place after I got hurt. Ask my sister. She'll tell you how I was a miserable asshole for almost a year. I couldn't put you through that." I tried to explain the best I could. There was no way to express into words how my mind and body turned on itself.

"You should have told me yourself. Back then. Not now." She turned her head to the side blocking me out. "Now, leave before I scream, and security shows up."

I reared back as if she slapped me. "Maybe I should scream, and we wait for security after the little stunt you pulled on me."

Her chin jutted out as she continued to look off to the side. "You can't prove anything."

Closing my eyes, I let out a heavy breath. "I'm sorry I hurt you, Dani. I really am, but you're better than this."

"You don't know me anymore. I've changed." Her jaw clenched and I knew then she was done. Dani could be stubborn as hell when she wanted to be, and she was right. I didn't know her anymore, but I wished I did. I desperately wanted to find out what happened to her. Why she was here and where was her healthy body?

"You're right I don't and maybe one day you'll give me a chance to know you again."

"Doubtful," she muttered, her eyes glassy.

I love you even after all this time.

"If you pull another prank or whatever it was you were doing earlier, I will remove you from the team." When she only blinked, I ground my teeth together. "Do you hear me?"

"Yes, Coach," she bit out. "Show yourself out."

I couldn't take my eyes off her as I left, wondering if she would say anything else or give me some indication of what was going on in her mind.

Had Dani been violated during our time apart?

The thought caused a pain in my stomach I'd never experience before. It was deep and raw as if it would eat me from the inside out. Maybe I should talk to her brother and see if he would tell me what happened. He wouldn't tell me shit. Not with Dani hating me the way she did.

She wanted me gone that was for certain. What I wanted to know was how she got my other key card and given it to Katie? Dani had turned devious, and if I didn't watch my back, she would have me kicked to the curb. What would I do then?

Luckily when I got back to my room it was vacant. I lost my shit earlier, and I knew it wouldn't be long before the entire team found out I lost my shit on Katie and the girls who showed up. I still couldn't believe Dani set me up like that knowing it would ruin my reputation.

Opening the minibar, I pulled out all the tiny bottles of alcohol ready to forget tonight. If I didn't, I'd never be able to fall asleep and I needed to have my head on straight for our first game. Tomorrow would set the precedent for the rest of the season. All eyes would be on me, on how well I had my team together.

There wasn't much to choose from. I was actually surprised the mini bar wasn't empty since we asked for all the rooms to not have access. First, we didn't want the girls drinking the night before, and second, we didn't want to foot the bill for all of them.

Picking the three whiskey bottles, I poured them into

a glass with a can of Sprite and drank it down faster than I would like to admit. If I would have had more in the bar, I would have drunk it all. Instead, I stripped out of my clothes and threw myself face down on the bed.

Dani's choked words of telling me to stop kept replaying in my head over and over again. I would never force myself on her or any woman. After an hour of lying there hoping the whiskey would tame the rioting going through my head, I picked up my phone and sent out one text message.

I'm sorry for ever hurting you. I would never force myself onto you, or into your life. I'll stay away until you're ready to talk.

IT DIDN'T SURPRISE me when I never received a message back. It was as it should be. Dani was supposed to be getting the sleep she needed for the game tomorrow. Still how could she possibly be sleeping after our encounter? After she thought I would take her by force.

Maybe I should go check on her and make sure she was okay. No, I shook my head against the pillow. I wasn't welcome in Dani's world right now, and maybe not ever. I only hoped she was getting more sleep than I was. At this rate, I was going to be bleary eyed and lost in my head for our first game with no sleep.

Climbing out of bed, I threw back the remaining bottles of alcohol in the fridge and hoped sleep would eventually find me before the sun came up.

NINE

DANICA

HOW WAS the only seat left on the bus directly across from Declan? If he planned this, I was going to expose the fact that Katie was in his bed last night. I didn't care that it wouldn't earn me any popularity points. I didn't want to be friends with these bitches anyway. The only reason they hated me was because I was better than all of them. Yes, I knew I seemed like a self-centered asshole, but there was a reason why I hadn't followed my twin to Willow Bay. They literally let anyone on the team even if they had zero soccer experience. They were that bad. I hated them because they reminded me of what I lost.

I threw my backpack down on the seat closest to Declan and sat with my back against the bus window. Lifting my head, I locked eyes with my coach. My eyes narrowed as I took in the dark circles under his eyes. During the game they were a light purple, but now they were nearly black.

"You look like shit."

"Be quiet," he hissed softly.

"I don't care if they hear me." Not that they would. Over half the girls on the bus had earbuds in, and the others were too far away from us. "Anyone who looks at you would think the same thing."

"Exactly. They'd think it, but they wouldn't say it to their coach. Words like that will get you benched." He tipped his head to me.

The corners of my mouth tip up. "Try it and see how well that works out for you."

Scooting to the edge of his seat, Declan leaned over into my space. "Are you blackmailing me?"

"I have plenty on you that I think the school would find interesting. Do you really think they'd want to keep you on as their head coach or a coach at all, knowing you've fucked one of their players?"

His brown eyes went wide, and his mouth went flat. "Jesus, Dani. You can't say that out loud."

"I sure as hell can. In fact, I just did." Leaning forward, I pressed my lips together to keep from laughing. Declan's body was rigid as his knee bounced. "What are you going to do about it?"

"I'm about to take you over my knee and spank the shit out of you. You may hate me for what I did to you, and I'll forever regret my actions toward you, but you must respect me as your coach."

"I don't take kindly to threats. You may want to rethink the way you talk to me."

Declan leaned back. His brows puckered in the center. "Who are you?"

"Your worst nightmare if you keep trying to fuck with my life." I turned to face the seat in front of me and put my own earbuds in as I pulled up Spotify to drown him and the rest of the world out.

SEVEN LONG AND tense hours later, we pulled up in front of our soccer stadium where the bus dropped us off. I was tired after hardly any sleep last night and from feeling Declan's presence so close to mine for the entire ride back. Even tired I had an immense desire to run and forget about everything, but I knew I couldn't do that. It would only lead to old patterns that would get me in trouble in the long run.

Stepping off the bus, I didn't say goodbye to a single soul as I started toward my house. I could have drove here yesterday, but I didn't want to leave my car here overnight. I was sure Oz and Lo would have been more than pleased to pick me up if I would have asked them, but I liked this alone time. While I liked going to and from practices with everyone, sometimes I just needed to be by myself out in the elements.

Instead of running, I thought about what food Ford likely left in the refrigerator while I was gone, and the homework I needed to finish since I didn't bring it along with me like I should have. It didn't take me long before I was opening the front door of the house. The guys were playing a game of Call of Duty or more like they were stomping West's ass because he sucked at it, but he was always a good sport about it when he played with them. Lo was in the kitchen with Charlie sitting by her feet as she pulled a bag of popcorn out of the microwave.

"Hey," she greeted me with a wide smile. She sat down the popcorn and hugged me. "How was the game?"

"We actually won," I murmured as I hugged her back.

She pulled back and held me by the arms. "Maybe it's a good thing *he's* the coach and did those tryouts." Lo had no idea of my plans for my ex and now coach, and I planned to keep it that way. I didn't want to see the look of disappointment in her eyes if she found out.

I couldn't argue that it was a good thing Declan had hosted the try outs. Otherwise, our team would probably never win a game. It didn't matter how good I was if the rest of the team was shit.

"You won?" Oz piped up from the living room.

Pulling away, I moved to the fridge to see what Ford had stocked us up with. "Yeah," I yelled back. "We might actually make it to the playoffs if yesterday was any indication."

"I'm sorry we couldn't go to the game," Oz's voice came from behind me before his long arms wrapped around my waist. He rested his cheek to the top of my head.

"I know how it goes. I hate it when I have to miss one of your games too, but travel isn't always conducive to our lives." Turning in his arms, I hugged him back. Our bond thrummed deep inside of me. God, I loved my brother. "I love you."

Oz hugged me harder. "I love you too, sis. Why don't you get yourself something to eat and then come join us kicking West's ass?"

I couldn't help but laugh. It wasn't how I planned my night to go, but once Oz offered, I couldn't find it in myself to deny him. It would be nice to kick back with them and have some fun knowing that they weren't worried about me. Or at least I didn't think they were.

Patting him on the back, I looked up at my twin. "Sounds like the perfect night."

We played for hours laughing and killing West over and over again. I couldn't remember the last time I had that much fun or felt this content. My belly was full, and my mind was at ease. I was ready to fall into my bed and sleep like the dead. That was until I stepped out of my steaming shower to hear Oz and Fin yelling. Don't get me wrong. They fought, but never like what I was hearing coming from the living room.

The bathroom door cracked open, and Lo peeked her head inside. Her blue eyes were wide as she frowned. "You may want to get out here. Declan showed up here furious and I think your brother may try to kill him."

Pulling my towel tighter around my body, I stomped down the hall. If Oz didn't kill Declan I would for interrupting my peaceful night. Tension grew in my stomach as I made my way into the living room. West was standing in front of the front door with one hand on Fin and Oz's chest as if he was holding them back.

"Thank god, you're out," West sighed. "You need to tell him not to show up here unless he's prepared to die. Although I don't think he'd care right now. He's equally pissed." West looked over his shoulder at the closed door. "I guess your plan worked."

"It didn't. Not really, so I don't know what he's doing here, but I'll take care of it."

I moved to step by them, but Oz hauled me back by my arm. "You're not going out there like that."

I jerked myself free. "Do you want me to take care of this or not before the neighbors call the cops because I can go back to my room and get dressed, but I think it would be wise for me to handle this now?"

Oz's nostrils flared, but he didn't stop me as I opened the front door and slipped outside. The night was warm, but had a breeze that sent goosebumps across my skin.

Declan stood at the far-left side of the porch with his fingers clutching his hair. The flex of his biceps had his shirt taut against his arms and broad back. Damn he was a fine specimen even if I did hate him.

Shaking myself out of my stupor, I crossed my arms over my chest holding my towel in place. All I needed was for it to slip and world war three to erupt outside. "What are you doing here? In case the last time wasn't an indicator, you're not welcome here."

Declan turned around eyes blazing and a deep frown marring his handsome face. He took one look at me and sank into the nearest chair. "What the hell happened to you?"

Widening my stance, I gripped the towel like I wanted to strangle his neck. "I think the better question is what happened to you? Why are you here all pissed off?"

"You had someone video tape her coming out of my room? What the hell were you thinking?"

"I wish I would have thought of that," I laughed, throwing my head back. "But unfortunately, I didn't. Looks like someone hates you as much as I do."

His head snapped up. "There's no reason for anyone else to hate me."

"At least you acknowledge there is a reason for me to hate you," I smirked at him, taking a step closer. "But I can think of a pretty good reason for a few people to hate you. You did kick five girls off the team," I informed him.

He stood and scoffed, crowding my space, but I stood my ground. "I didn't kick them off. They didn't make the team. Plain and simple."

I had to hold back a laugh at that. Everything wasn't as black and white as he liked to make them seem.

"It doesn't mean it didn't piss anyone off or make them sad. How did you feel when your career was over?" I whispered into the night's air.

"Those girls were never going to have a career as soccer players." His voice was devoid of all emotion. He didn't care about any of the girls on the team. His hands went to his hips making him stand like Superman. Any other time I would've thought it was funny, but not then.

"Neither am I, and it kills me each time I think about it. They were on the team and now they're not. It doesn't matter if they weren't going to make it or not. Their reality has changed and you're an easy target. Plain and simple."

Declan took a step closer making me take a step back. "Your career doesn't have to be over. I still don't understand why you left UCLA to play here." He reached out and dropped his hand at the last minute.

"Because I was starving myself for them," I shouted before I swung around and escaped inside.

TEN

DECLAN

I WASN'T sure how long I stood in the same spot running over Dani's words in my mind over and over again. What did she mean she was starving herself? How? Why would she do that to herself?

It took everything in me to not pound on their front door and demand for Danica to come back out here and answer my questions, but I knew I didn't have that right. She had no reason to answer any of my questions. No matter how desperately I wanted to know the answers.

I wasn't sure how long I stood there before my feet finally unglued from the ground and started for my car. The entire drive was a blur as I thought about how Dani and I were together before I left for Spain. She told me everything from her dreams to her fears as we laid in bed for hours at a time. I knew each and every name of the people in the house I had just left, and how she never thought her best friend would be the same after she was raped their sophomore year. What I wouldn't give for her to open up to me again and tell me what happened while I was gone.

Pulling my phone out of my pocket once I parked my car in my garage, I stared at it for a long time before I opened my messages app and pulled up Dani's name.

I'm sorry.

SHE DIDN'T RESPOND. Not that I expected her to. The only thing I could do now was prove to her how sorry I was, and hope eventually she'd forgive me enough to open up to me.

Even with no sleep the night before, sleep alluded me once again. Danica's body in that towel flashed behind my eyelids over and over again. While normally it would get me hard, the way her collarbones jutted out from the top of the towel had me wondering just how skinny she got before she left LA.

I barely got more than a few hours of sleep before it

was time for practice on Monday. I sipped the last of my coffee as the first girl stepped onto the field.

"Hey, Coach," she called before she started to stretch.

I tipped my chin in her direction as I watched the team trickle out onto the field, waiting for the one player I wanted to see most. Dani was the last to arrive like she was to almost every practice. It couldn't be easy to have no friends on the team. The only people Dani had were the ones she lived with as far as I knew.

She didn't look at me as she started to stretch as far away from me as possible.

"Today's practice is going to be different. We're going to split up into two groups and play against each other for the first half, and after that we're going to watch footage of Saturday's game. If I touch your shoulder, move to the right side of field and come up with a strategy. For the others—"

"To the left," they answered as one. At least they were finally turning into a team.

"That's what I'm talking about. I'm so proud of the way you're finally becoming a team and working together. The more that happens the better we'll become." I clapped my hands. "Now line up."

I already knew who I wanted on each team. It wasn't easy to find the perfect mixture where they'd focus on the game and not who they were playing with. When I got to

Dani and went to touch her, she leaned back out of the way. My stomached dropped that she couldn't even stand my touch when she once craved it.

An hour later, we all stepped foot into the viewing room. The girls sipped on waters and Gatorades while they slumped down in their chairs. I'd already watched the footage five times since I couldn't sleep the night before. I might have watched it because it was the only footage I had of Dani, and since she was the star of the game, she was featured in it the most.

Instead of taking the seat closest to me, Dani sat on the floor with her back against the wall and her legs out in front of her as she touched her toes. Her chest rested against her thighs as she leaned into the stretch.

I wanted to demand that she get off the floor, but I wasn't going to use my power against her. It would only harden her against me more. Instead, I turned on the film and watched it with everyone else like it was my first time. I had the entire game memorized at that point. Every few minutes, I'd look over at Dani to find her engrossed in the footage. She would make a damn fine coach one day if she wanted to.

Stopping the footage of the first half, I leaned back in my chair. "Do any of you see any opportunities we could have made to make the game better?"

"Karrie should have blocked that shot," one of the girls piped up.

"Yeah," Karrie said softly. "Sorry. I'll work on it."

"Anything else?" There were a few more little things, but for the most part they played their hearts out and were damn good.

"Danica needs to learn how to share the ball." Number nine sneered. It was my bad I didn't know all of their names yet, but she was one of the least talented players and didn't play much.

Out of the corner of my eye, I saw Dani stiffen. "Why, so you can give it up when I share it with you?" She spat back.

"All right ladies." I stood and stalked around the room. "This is a team, and you're going to act like it. Danica will give you more opportunities with the ball." I wanted to say if they all stopped being bitches to her, but I held that back. That wasn't professional, and it showed I knew her more than the others. They all knew we both played for UCLA and attended at the same time, but if they knew we dated it would be career suicide. I couldn't even imagine how they'd treat Dani if they knew. Not that I showed any favoritism. In fact, I tried to keep my interaction with her limited on and off the field. Although I would like to change the latter.

She looked well rested today and had run laps around

the rest of her teammates. I guess our talk didn't affect her like it had done me.

Danica's eyes narrowed at me as she crossed her arms over her chest, but she didn't argue with me. She knew she had to be a team player even if there was no one else that could even remotely match her abilities on the field.

"Let's watch the last half and see if we can find any room for improvement. Then we're going to watch footage of the Wolves, and come up with a strategy against them."

"Isn't that his job," one of the girls whispered too loudly.

I opened my mouth to speak, but it was Dani who spoke first. "This is a team, right? Then act like it. You should be honored that Coach Hart is letting you in on this level."

"Kiss ass," someone said before a few of the girls snickered.

"If you can't get along in here then how in the hell are you going to be a united front out there on the field?" I barked my question out. I knew I couldn't make them like Dani, but they sure as hell could respect her.

I started the film back up and walked around the room. When I got by Dani, I squatted down beside her. "You don't need to stick up for me. I can handle a group of girls."

"Oh, I bet you can," she said between clenched teeth. "And don't worry that will be the last time I defend you. It doesn't do any good anyways." She shrugged and went back to watching the film.

She was right, it didn't. I wasn't sure what it was about the girls here, but they just didn't seem to get along with each other unless it was to gang up on Dani or me. Maybe the girls here were all snobby ass bitches. The new girls had formed a clique and had left Dani out of it. Or maybe she had left herself out of it. I wasn't sure. Maybe she didn't want any friends, or maybe she was torturing herself in a new way.

"Can I talk to you after practice?" I asked before I stood up. I couldn't be seen talking to her for too long. I didn't want the girls to think I favored Dani more than them even if it was the truth. That's why I pushed her so hard during practice. I would do everything in my power to make her the best she could be, and possibly get her seen for the chance to make it to the Olympics in two years.

Her gaze flicked to mine. "Do I have to?"

"You don't have to do anything you don't want to, but eventually I would like to talk to you." I didn't wait for her response. Instead, I went back to my seat and kept my eyes on the film. It was always difficult to keep my eyes off of Dani, but I did my best. Did I fail?

Most definitely. At least five times, but I was getting better.

When we were finished, I waited not so patiently to see if Dani would stick around, but she was one of the first out of the room. I thought maybe just maybe she would come back once they were all gone, but twenty minutes after everyone had cleared out, I was still alone.

It took all my strength to keep myself from driving over to her house and confronting her with the information she gave me the last time. I wasn't sure how long I'd be able to keep myself away. I'd always been drawn to Dani, and now was no exception. Except now the need to save her was overwhelming.

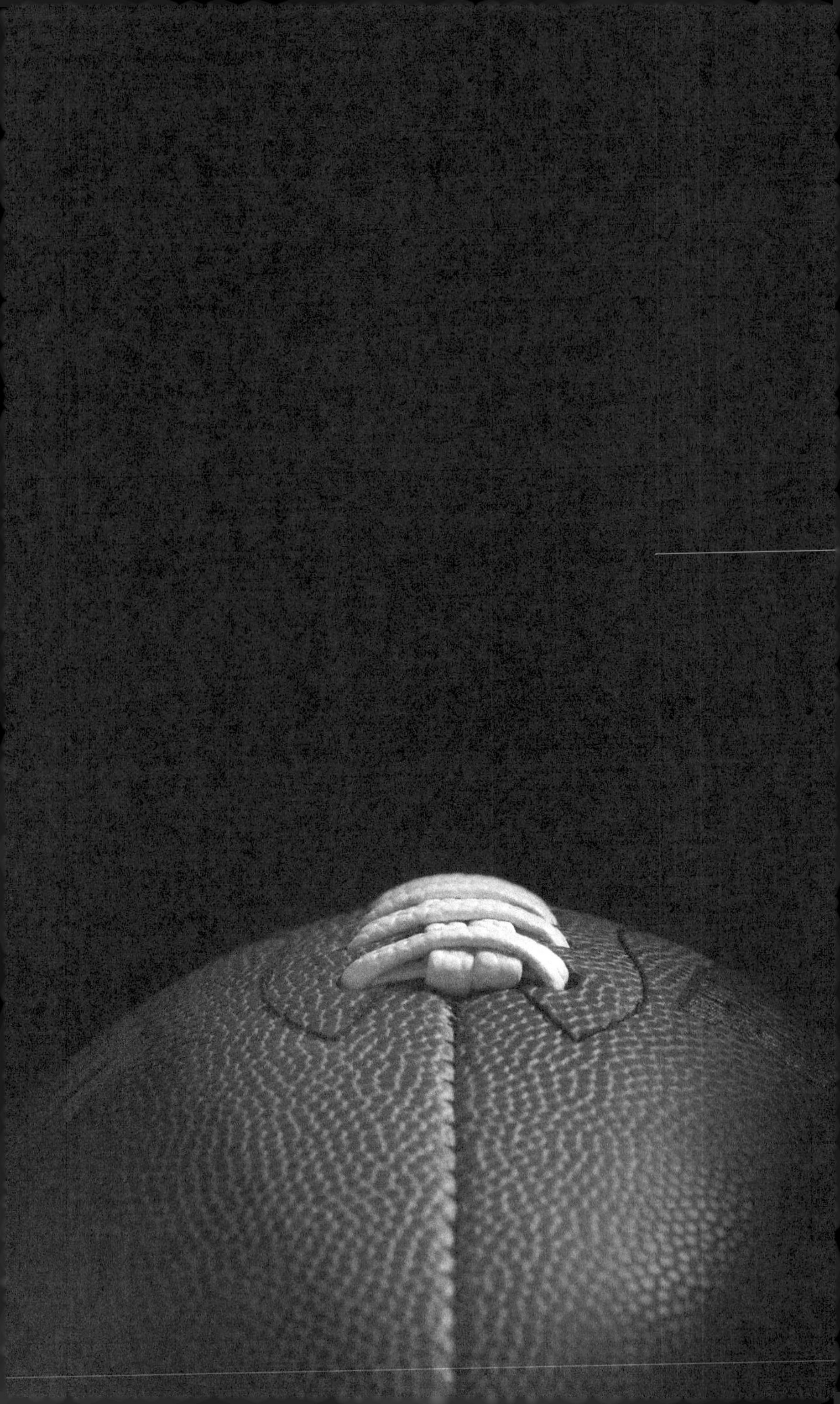

ELEVEN

DANICA

IF HE THOUGHT I didn't know he was looking at me, Declan had another thing coming. He'd been staring at me out of the corner of his eye for the last twenty minutes. It was unnerving. It had been like this all week. It made me *almost* wish I'd stuck around to see what he wanted to say to me the other day. The keyword here was almost. I didn't want to talk to Declan about what I let slip out when he unexpectedly showed up. Again.

"Are you ready to beat the Wolves?" He shouted, clapping his hands.

"Yes," we roared back at him, stomping our feet.

"That's what I want to hear. Now let's get out there and kick some…"

"Ass," we supplied for him, and then all laughed at the shocked look on his face.

Coach Perry whispered in his ear, and red-hot jealousy shot down my spine. I didn't like the way I was feeling one bit. He smiled and nodded before turning back to us.

"I wasn't sure if I could say ass," he chuckled. "Now let's get out there and kick some Wolf ass."

"Yeah!" We lined up and jogged out onto the field. It was strange, but we had become more of a team this last week. Maybe the rest of them actually listened to Declan, or maybe they knew that if they weren't bitches to me, I might pass them the ball more often. Whatever it was, I liked it. That didn't mean I was going to become besties with any of them. Still if we could happily work together, I would do my best not to ice them out on the field.

WITH MY HEAD DOWN, I gritted my teeth. My instep was killing me. I'd taken a nasty blow to the top of my foot during the last two minutes of the game. I couldn't wait to get to my room, and get some ice on it.

"Are you sure you're, okay?" Ashley asked as she walked in the hotel beside me.

"I'll be fine by tomorrow." I tried to smile, but I knew I failed as a flash of pain heated my entire body.

"Do you need help to your room? I can get your bag."

I was sure she had a hopeful look on her face, but I couldn't bring myself to look.

"I'm—

"I've got it," Declan interrupted with my bag already on his shoulder.

"You don't need to do that." He was the last person I wanted help from.

"Actually, I do. Now, let's get you up to your room and take a good look at your foot now that a little more time has gone by."

It was bad. I already knew that. When it happened, it was already an angry shade of red. Now it was swollen. I could barely get a sock on after the game. I'd be lucky to play in the next game since it was only three days away.

I didn't argue with him where everyone could hear. Once we were safely in my room away from prying ears, I'd kick him out.

"They should have given you crutches to keep the weight off," he mumbled by my side. He moved to my right side, and I braced for his touch.

"Come on Dani. It's not going to kill you," he said softly enough for only me to here.

"You don't know that," I whisper-yelled as I let him take some of my weight. His smell came rushing through my senses. God, he smelled good. I could never place what it was though. It was a strange mix of cologne and outdoors that was unique to only him.

"Everyone is to be in their rooms by ten o'clock and not to leave until daylight. I'll be coming to each of your rooms to check, so don't think that you can be late. There will be an extra practice for those who think they can get one over on us."

Coach Perry nodded along with him. It made me wonder why she couldn't help me to my room. Didn't it seem suspect to anyone?

"Alright, you all have your keys, so you can go," Coach Perry spoke. She was quiet most of the time. Half the time I forgot she was around until she was yelling at us on the field. Still, I liked her. Too bad she wasn't escorting me up.

Since we were all on the same floor, the majority of us got on the first two elevators and got off together. I hobbled to my room with Declan's help where he promptly took my card from me and opened the door like I was an invalid.

Luckily the bed wasn't too far in, and I could escape being so close to Declan. It was hard to push away the memories when all I wanted to do was bury my nose into his chest and get lost.

"I'll be right back with some ice."

Before I could protest, Declan was out the door with

my ice bucket in hand. Pulling my duffle bag closer, I dug through it until I found my bottle of ibuprofen and shook out three little pills. I threw them back before I started to peel my sock off my swollen and sore foot. I knew the pain relievers weren't going to kick in that quickly, but hopefully they'd eventually help. The ones I'd been given before never seemed to work. I was hoping that was because they were defective, and it wasn't because there was something more seriously wrong with my foot. I wouldn't know for sure until Monday when I went to the doctor.

Declan slipped inside my room with the bucket of ice in his hands. It brought back memories of him sneaking into my room after games when he'd come to see me. Damn, did I miss those days when everything was easier. Back then I had no idea how easy I had it.

"Sorry, that took so long. I was ambushed out in the hall." I swore his cheeks pinked up as he ducked inside the bathroom to grab a towel. Did he like one of the other girls?

"Well, don't let me stop you from having a good time." I ripped the towel from his hands only for him to take it back just as quickly.

He shook his head as he got down on one knee and carefully removing my sock since I hadn't got it past my ankle yet. "Don't be…" he shook his head and blew out a loud breath through his nose. "I have zero interest in any of the girls on the team, and that would be highly unprofessional."

I narrowed my eyes at him even though he wasn't looking. All of his attention was on my foot as he oh so carefully removed my sock. "So is you being in my room. Coach Perry could easily be here helping me."

"Well, I'm the head coach and what I say goes, and I said I would help you and I meant it. Now stop being difficult," he snapped.

"Ouch," I grumbled. Looking down, I saw he'd gotten my sock off. Had he been trying to distract me? My foot looked horrible. It was already a dark shade of purple and the entire middle was swollen.

"Sorry. I tried to make it as pain free as possible." He tapped the side of my leg. "Scoot back on the bed. Your foot should be propped up." I did as I was instructed, strangely turned on by his demands even if I did still hate him. With rapt attention, I watched as he laid the towel out on the bed and scooped ice out of the bucket and placed it on the towel. The way his long nimble fingers moved as Declan took care of me had my nether regions catching fire. It didn't matter though, my heart still hurt.

"Where were you when I needed you most?" It slipped out before I could stop it.

Declan faltered. A lone ice cube fell to the floor as his

eyes trained on me. With one look at me they became glassy. "I'm sorry I wasn't. If I would have known maybe it would have pulled me out of my funk. Dani," his voice cracked on my name. "I would do anything for you."

"Would you leave right now if I asked you?"

He swallowed and nodded. "If that's what you need." He licked his bottom lip and placed the makeshift ice pack on my foot. "First, will you tell me what happened? I've barely been able to sleep since you told me you were starving yourself. How did my brave, strong Danica do this to herself?"

Because I was no longer yours.

I didn't say it though, no matter how much I wanted to. It wasn't only on him. In fact, it was all on me for being weak and letting those around me control me.

"Please," he begged.

"Can you… I don't want to look at you when I tell you." Hell, I didn't want to tell him at all, but I knew he'd never give up until I spilled every last detail.

"Why?" his eyes pleaded with me for answers.

"Because I'm ashamed, and I don't want to see the look on your face when I tell you what happened." I took in a sharp intake of air which did nothing to settle my nerves. "You just called me strong and brave, and I was neither of those things. I'm still not, and I'm not sure I ever will be again."

"To me you are." With that he turned his back to me. Placing his elbows on his knees, he clasped his hands together and waited for me to start.

God, why was I going to spill my inner most demons to this man? Maybe it was to hurt him the way he hurt me. So that he would know his hand in my demise.

"You know my sophomore year without Lo by my side was more than difficult for me. I wasn't the most accepting of her relationship with my brother, and I should have been for both their sakes." My lower lip quivered as I thought about how happy they were now, and how they suffered because of me.

"I know," he whispered, bowing his head.

"We were good. You got me through that even if you didn't realize it. I loved you even if I didn't tell you." I sucked in a breath, and held it until my chest felt as if it was going to explode. "Maybe if I would have told you, you wouldn't have shut me out and eventually blocked me." I chuckled without humor at my next words. "I thought you loved me, but that was just a fantasy world I was living in."

Declan jerked and then turned around. His brown eyes filled with so much sadness it nearly broke my heart. "I did love you. Hell, I still do, Dani. I was selfish for shutting you out. I did it to everyone in my life and looking back, I wish I wouldn't have. Damn, I'm sorry."

He bit his bottom lip and tugged it between his teeth. "And I'm hijacking the moment. Go ahead."

Did his words make me feel better? Slightly, but it still didn't make up for the pain he caused.

Wrapping my arms around my knees, I started to pick at my toenail polish on my uninjured foot as I spoke. My other foot was almost completely numb of the pain from earlier. Tomorrow it would hurt like a bitch, but tonight another pain was taking over. "I won't lie. I wasn't in a good place when you cut off contact. I was vulnerable in a way that I've never been before." I would never put myself in a position to leave myself bare to anyone again.

"I'm the cause of this?" He choked out.

"Not in the way you think." Clutching my toes, I closed my eyes as the back of my eyes started to sting. There was no way I was going to let Declan see me cry. I wanted to put the ice pack on my brain to numb the thoughts that came rushing back. "My coaches told me I needed to lose weight."

"Not even an ounce. Especially not now, but even not then. Your body was beautiful."

It didn't escape my notice that he used the past tense.

"I believed them." I shrugged one shoulder as a lump started to form in my throat. "I thought maybe that's why you left and wanted nothing to do with me."

Declan scooted forward, placing his hand on top of mine. "You know why I left."

"I do, but at the time, I was confused as to why you cut off contact. All I wanted to do was make sure you were okay. Do you know how much it hurt me to find out you were injured from the internet? I had people asking me how you were doing, and my choice was either to lie or say I didn't know." A tear slipped down my cheek and trailed to my knee.

"I'm so sorry."

"Just let me say this. It doesn't help to know what you felt."

"No, you're right. What matters is how you felt."

At least we could agree on that one thing.

"At first, I thought it would just be a few pounds. I cut back on my food, ran more, and did more weight training. I did look better in the beginning, but then they asked for more. I can't say they wanted me to be unhealthy. Maybe they wanted me to put on more muscle. I don't know."

It was all becoming too much. Thinking about how I'd been back then. Lying down on the bed, I curled into myself, needing to feel whole and protected.

"I started to run more. When my feet were pounding on the concrete, track, or wherever else I found myself, I forgot about all my problems. Essentially, I substituted running for what most people would do with alcohol or drugs. I became addicted. The more I ran, the more I wasn't hungry, and then it all became a very vicious cycle."

"What about your family?" He asked, his voice rough with emotion, one I didn't want to put too much stock into. I didn't have it in me.

"Oh, they noticed, and I lied to them. I was too far gone by the time they saw me. I didn't want to stop. Running and not eating were two things I could control in my otherwise chaotic life. When my parents demanded I get help, I fought them every step of the way, but then Oz came to me, and…" Pain ripped through my chest remembering how broken my twin brother looked when he saw me for the first time since Christmas. "I lied to my family and said I was busy. Oz knew something was wrong, but he had his own problems to deal with. I don't think he ever thought I'd lie to him, but I did. I lied to everyone including myself." I wasn't sure when the tears had started relentlessly flowing down my cheeks, but my pillow was wet, and my nose was running. "I got treatment over the summer and then moved in with my brother, Lo, and his friends."

The room was quiet for several long minutes. I wasn't even sure if Declan was still there. Truthfully, I would have been happy if he had left because then I knew I wouldn't have to deal with him. Maybe he wanted nothing to do with me now that he knew I wasn't the strong girl he pictured me being.

The bed dipped and in the next second, I was pulled into Declan's strong arms. I didn't even try to fight him. Instead, I had to fight to keep from turning around and burying my face into his chest.

"Fuck, Dani. I'm so damn sorry. You'll never know how badly I feel right now. To know that I had a hand in something that could have taken your life." His breath hitched. "I'm not sure I'll ever be able to forgive myself knowing that if I would have been brave enough to pick up the phone, none of this would have happened." His grip on me tightened.

While I liked to blame Declan for all of my problems, he was only the catalyst. No one forced me into doing anything I didn't want to do.

He pressed his forehead into the back of my head. His voice was barely more than a whisper as he spoke. "Now it makes sense why you're here."

"Yeah, I have a house full of babysitters. One of their roommates moved out so I could move in. He's becoming a chef and he cooks for all of us, but he's really just trying to put some more meat on my bones."

"You need it. Don't fight them over it."

"I'm not, but it's hard. Even though it was a relatively

short period of time compared to many others before they got treatment it's still difficult. Somehow, someway my brain got hardwired differently." All of a sudden, I was exhausted. Opening up to Declan wrecked me, and all I wanted to do was sleep.

In the back of my mind, I knew I should have kicked Declan out of my room, but for the first time since all of this began, I felt as if I was where I was supposed to be. I only hoped I didn't regret it in the morning.

TWELVE
DECLAN

WAKING up in bed with Dani was a dream come true, but not under the circumstances of last night. I was sure she wouldn't be happy with how it all played out once she woke up. Her words kept playing on repeat over and over again in a torturous loop.

It killed me to know I had any part in herself destruction. My beautiful, strong girl fell apart without me by her side. I didn't blame her for hating me. I hated myself. I wasn't sure I'd ever forgive myself for shutting her out. If only I would have picked up the phone when she called or reached out, our lives would be so different right now. Only I couldn't say Dani would be in my life in this moment. She would still be in Los Angeles, and I would be… I had no idea.

I wanted to go back to Danica's room and beg for

forgiveness, but now wasn't the time. I had crept out like a coward, afraid of what her reaction would be when she woke up in my arms. It didn't escape me that she sunk deep into my arms like she never left or how quickly she fell asleep. After four hours of listening to her breath and luxuriating in the feel of her body flush to mine, I pried myself away from the one person I wanted to have by my side for the rest of my life. It nearly killed me to do it, but what would have hurt worse was her rejection of me when she woke up.

My phone trilled letting me know someone was trying to FaceTime me. My sister Roxie's name flashed on the screen. I didn't want to answer, but I knew I had to, or she would continue to call me over and over again until I picked up and there was no way in hell I was having any conversation with her on the bus with all those girls around.

"Hey, Rox," I answered trying to pretend my world was right when everything felt so wrong in the moment.

Her smile fell and she chocked her head to the side. "You look like shit. Are you still not sleeping?"

"Wow, no small talk just straight into hounding me?" I tried to laugh it off, but was unsuccessful.

Her face softened, and I heard her boyfriend, Merrick, say something in the background. "I'm sorry. You know I worry about you."

I did know. If it weren't for Roxie, I wasn't sure where I'd be. She was the one who made me pull my head out of my ass, and force me to see my life wasn't over when my career was cut short in the first few months of my career beginning.

"I don't mean to cause you any worry. You should be happily living your life and making me an uncle."

Roxie spit out the coffee she was drinking and laughed. "I don't think we're quite ready for that stage in our lives yet."

"Why not? You'd be the best mom ever." While she would, I was deflecting her attention off me. It was always easy when it was about her live-in boyfriend. "Listen I need to go. We have to be on the bus in twenty minutes and I still need to take a shower."

Her mouth curved down. "Okay, yeah. I'll let you go. I was just calling to congratulate you on your win last night since I didn't hear from you." She looked down and then her lips twitched. "In fact, I need to get out of here myself. I have a class to teach in an hour. Let's do dinner this weekend or something."

"Yeah," I agreed because it was easier than saying no. Roxie would be back to hounding me about not sleeping. I'd find some excuse as to why I couldn't make dinner.

"I love you, little bro." She smiled wickedly knowing how much I hated her calling me that. Not because I was almost a foot taller than her, but because she'd always had a complex growing up since she wasn't stick thin like all the other girls. Luckily now with Merrick, she was finally seeing how beautiful she was. That's why I overlooked she had been sleeping with her student. A fact she hid from me until they were caught. Her lying to me still didn't sit well with me. I guess I knew how she felt since I hadn't opened up to her about why I was having so many sleepless nights. At least he wasn't her student any longer. He graduated last year, so that was a plus.

"Love you too. I'll see you later in the week." I disconnected the call and let out a sigh. I was going to have to tell her about Dani. Not all of it because that was Dani's story to tell, but about my guilt.

I wondered if the pain in my chest and the guilt would ever go away.

I was the first on the bus. I sat in the back in order to watch over the girls. Yes, they were adults, but they didn't act like it much of the time. They fought like cats and dogs to the point they felt like elementary children. It was getting better though. With each passing day and win, they were became more of a team. If it kept going like this, it could lead them to a championship.

Unlike most days, Dani wasn't last to everything team related. She was one of the first few on the bus. She hobbled on and I instantly felt bad. I should have gone to her to see if she needed help, but I was too in my head. Instead of me, it was one of the girls. Dani plopped down in the first seat, and I immediately wanted to get up and go to her. But I couldn't do anything except sit on my ass and yearn to be by her side.

Once all the girls were on the bus, and distracted with trying to either go back to sleep or listening to whatever was playing on their headphones, I pulled out my phone and brought up Dani's name. I wasn't sure if she'd unblocked me yet. She'd never once responding to any one of my text messages, but even still I sent her another one.

**I'm sorry I wasn't there when you woke up.
I wanted to be, but wasn't sure how you'd feel.
It should have been me helping you on the bus.**

DANI DIDN'T RESPOND. Not that I expected her to. From where I was sitting, I couldn't tell what she was doing. All I could see was the very top of her blonde head which I kept my eyes on the entire bus ride back to Willow Bay. I should have slept, but that was unprofessional unless it was an overnight driving trip, or at least I thought so. Plus, I didn't want to talk in my sleep or wake up from a nightmare with over two dozen girls staring at me.

Time went by quickly for once, and before I knew it, we were pulling up outside our locker room. The girls all filed out of the bus eager to get back home. All but Dani and one other girl who was trying to help Danica.

"Don't worry about it, Kourtney. I'll help Dani off. Thank you for trying to help."

Kourtney gave me a small smile before she turned to Dani. "I hope your foot feels better soon. We need you."

"Oh, I'm not going anywhere. I'm going to baby this thing as much as possible."

"We'll see what the doctor says," I grumbled. There was no way I was going to let her play if the doctor told her to stay off it. Not even if she begged.

Dani's blue eyes narrowed as she turned to me. "Are you going to help me get off this bus or not?"

Kourtney gasped before she quickly left the bus.

The impulse to sweep Dani up in my arms was almost too much to ignore. I probably would have if half the team wasn't still in the parking lot.

"I'm going to help, you just need to be patient. If not, I'm going to pick you up and carry you off this bus."

Her eyes flared. "Let's not do that."

"Yeah, I didn't think so," I chuckled. "Can you put any weight on your foot?"

"Some but navigating stairs is a little tough. I think I sweated more getting up those damn stairs earlier than I did through the entire game yesterday."

I hummed as I thought about the easiest way to get her off the bus without hurting her. "Maybe we should take you to the doctor today before it gets any worse?"

"I'll be fine once I get home. There's bound to be a pair of crutches around there I can use."

"Why don't you find out and we'll go from there?" I helped her to stand even though I knew she didn't need my assistance, and then placed my arm around her waist. The main problem was the bus aisle and stairs were narrow. It wasn't made for two people to be side by side, so we had to improvise by shuffling sideways.

"Could this be more awkward?" Dani muttered as I helped her down the last step. I grabbed her waist and then sat her down on the pavement.

"I'm sorry. There really should be training for this, or we need a bigger bus."

"I opt for both," she answered back with a grimace.

"Are you okay?"

"Yeah, I'll be fine. I was just wondering how I'm going to drive home." She sighed heavily. Her brows furrowed as she looked out into the distance. "I should have had someone drop me off, but I didn't want to bother them with picking me up."

"I can drive you home and we can figure out a way to get your car."

Dani pressed her lips together. "That's probably not the best idea. If my brother sees me pull up with you, he'll probably kill you first and ask questions after."

I didn't blame him. If anyone hurt Roxie the way I hurt Danica, I would want to kill them as well. "It probably won't help, but I'd like the opportunity to apologize."

Dani bit down on her bottom lip as she stared up at me. "I don't know." She looked around the parking lot and then back up at me when she saw there was no one else around. "Why would you want to do that?"

I wasn't sure if she was ready for my answer, but I gave it to her anyway. "Because I hope to be a part of your life."

"I'm not sure I'm ready for that." She shook head and looked down.

"Hey," I whispered, emotion clogging in my throat. Placing my index finger under her chin, I slowly lifted her head until her eyes locked with mine. "I don't want to push you, but I also need you to know what I want. I want you back in my life as more than just your coach. I want to be able to hold your hand and have you in my bed each night."

"That can't happen," she blurted out, her eyes wide. "Like you said, you're my coach. We can't be out holding hands in public."

"Did I say in public?" I chuckled, deflecting. This was becoming a habit I needed to break.

"Stop," she chastised me. "But seriously Declan, I'm not sure I'm ready for you. I'm still so messed up, and ninety percent of the time I hate you."

"Well, maybe we can hang out during those other ten percent." I tried to smile, but it dropped immediately. I'd put myself out there and been turned down, but what did I expect?

"Yeah, maybe." She chewed on the inside of her cheek. I was making her nervous in a way I didn't want. "Is your offer to drive me home still available or should I call my brother?"

"I'll take you wherever you want to go." Wrapping my arm around her waist to help her to my car, I tried to think of a way to make things right between us, but I knew there was no easy fix. Only time would heal her wounds. Helping her inside my car, I threw our bags into the backseat before slipping behind the steering wheel.

Pressing the ignition, I gripped the steering wheel before I spoke. "I'm sorry, Dani. If I could rewind time I would. Instead, the only thing I can do is kill those fucking coaches for ever suggesting you needed to lose even an ounce of weight."

Her small, warm hand gripped my bouncing knee. "Don't. They're not worth you going to prison over."

"They might not be, but you sure as hell are. I'd do anything for you."

"Then let them live and don't give them any headspace. You're better than that."

Was I, though?

Her grip tightened on my knee. "But thank you for wanting to defend me. It means a lot."

"You mean everything to me, Dani. I'm sorry I ever made you feel differently. I'll try to prove that to you until my dying breath."

THIRTEEN
DANICA

LYING IN BED, I couldn't get Declan's words out of my head. How was I considering letting him back in my life when he nearly ruined me before? I wasn't sure, but I was.

Maybe it was because I was lonely. And horny. Everyone in my house had someone. Even Ford when he came over to cook for us or drop off our meals. They were all in love, and I was the third wheel wherever we went. It didn't help that I hadn't had sex with anyone else since Declan. I was sure he'd slept with half of Spain while he was there. The thought had me wanting to scratch his eyes out and rip off his dick. Maybe I should ask him. Once he told me how many women he'd been with, I could firmly put him back into the hate category.

How many women have you been with since me?

IMMEDIATELY THE THREE dots started to bounce up and down.

None

> **Now, I know you're lying.**

I promise I'm not.

> **Okay. How many women have you had sex with?**

IF HE WAS GOING to make me come out and outright ask, I would. There was no way in hell Declan had gone over a year without sex. If I hadn't been so messed up in the head and trying to lose every ounce I could, I would have been at the bars or frat houses trying to pick up every guy I could. With Declan's good looks there was no way he'd made it this long without sex.

. . .

Zero.

You're a fucking liar.
Thanks for that. Good night.

I promise I'll never lie to you.
The only person I've been with is my hand.
If I'm lying, then my dick can fall off.

It's probably going to fall off because of the STD
you got in Spain.

If I got tested, would you believe me?

I'm pretty sure there's no test for how long it's been
since you last got your dick wet.

How CAN I prove it to you?

THERE WAS no way in hell Declan could prove to me he'd been celibate this entire time. It didn't make sense.

WHY DON'T you come by my place, and we can talk?

I'll answer any questions you have for me.

Why your place?

BECAUSE I'M PRETTY SURE your brother won't take kindly to me showing up on your doorstep again.

I'm not sure I can get away.
Where would I say I'm going?

THE LIBRARY? I don't know.

Why tell them anything?

**It's kind of like jail here.
I never go anywhere without them unless it's a
game.**

DAMN THAT DIDN'T SOUND good, but it was true. I had become reliant on Oz, Fin, and West. They were probably tired of having to entertain me and make sure I ate.

Send me your address. I'll be over in thirty.

RIGHT THEN I decided it was time I started to live my life and so should my roommates. I was fine. I would never let Declan break and ruin me again. I was in charge of my destiny, and it was time to get out of my sheltered world.

Slipping on a t-shirt over my sports bra and a pair of slides, I looked down at myself. It wasn't sexy, but who cared. Declan saw me in something like this five days a week. Grabbing my backpack, I slung it over my shoulder and headed out of my room. I didn't want to lie, but I had no idea what to say to Oz either. He wouldn't approve of me going to see Declan, and I understood why. Still, I needed to do this. I needed to live.

Oz and Lo looked up from the movie they were watching on the couch as I walked into the room. I breathed a sigh of relief it was only them. Fin would have probably given me the inquisition. The only problem was Oz always knew when I was lying. At least when there wasn't a hundred miles or more separating us.

He tilted his head to the side and took me in. "Where are you going?"

"I'm..." I looked to Lo and then back to him, unsure of what to say.

"She's going out. Don't you remember she has that big test on Wednesday?"

"Oh, yeah. Sorry." He paused their movie. His mouth turned down as he looked at the remote. "Are we being too loud?"

"No, you're fine. I wanted a change of scenery, and to get out of the house." All true, but not the whole story either.

"Okay." He blew out a breath. "Good luck studying."

"Thanks. I'm not sure how long I'll be gone." I almost

said more, but I didn't want to lie. They could assume whatever they wanted though.

Lo leaned her head on Oz's shoulder and smiled up at me. Did she know what I was going to do?

"You don't have to answer to me. You're your own person. I just want to make sure you're safe. If you need me for anything. I mean *anything*, you let me know. Day or night. I don't care when it is. Okay?"

"I promise." And I meant it. I wouldn't shut Oz or Lo out of my life again. It was too easy to fall back into old habits if I did. Not that I thought I would.

Oz nodded and flashed me a smile. "Grab yourself a snack. Ford made these incredible hickory smoked almonds that are to die for."

"They're addictive." Lo leaned forward and grabbed a couple out of a bowl and threw them in her mouth. "I could eat that entire bowl in one sitting. There actually might not be any more left when you get home if you don't get some now."

"Okay. I'm intrigued." I picked one up and the second I started to chew, I moaned, closing my eyes. I opened my eyes wide. "Damn, those might be my new favorite thing."

"I know, right? I seriously haven't been able to stop eating them. Do me a favor and take some. When you see how many of them are in the kitchen you'll understand."

I laughed and backtracked to the kitchen. There was a large bag on the counter filled with almonds. Damn, Ford was too good to us. There was no denying he was most definitely going to an amazing chef one day. Everyone would know who he was. There was no other way about it. Me and everyone else in the house were grateful we had him cooking for us on the regular. I wasn't sure if he would still be cooking for them as much as he was if I wasn't here. Still, I appreciated the fact that he continued for me. He always made me the most delicious food that was impossible to deny.

My stomach clenched in knots wondering if I was making the right decision to go see Declan. What if he said something and it set me back? I wasn't sure I could hear about all the women he slept with since he left to play in Spain. He cheated on me and that was why it was so easy for him to shut me out? It wasn't the first time the thought popped into my head. Declan didn't seem like a cheater, but he also didn't seem like the type of guy who would stop calling me and block me from any type of communication either.

Picking out a little storage container, I filled it with almonds, and shoved it in my backpack. "I'll see you guys later. Enjoy your movie." I waved as I walked past them.

"Thanks," Lo called back. "We should do a chick flick night the next time the guys have an away game."

"Count me in." I waved and shut the door quickly behind me before they decided to ask any more questions. I had my own to ask. I'd opened up to Declan and now it was his turn to spill his soul out on the table and answer all the questions that had been percolating in my head for over a year.

I checked my phone to see an address that according to my GPS would only take me ten minutes to drive to. Since I rarely drove myself around Willow Bay, I had no idea where most things were. Instead of driving like my usual speed demon self, I drove slowly as I tried to calm my nerves.

Twelve minutes later, I pulled up in front of a one-story Mediterranean style house. It wasn't what I was expecting from Declan. I guess I thought it would be an apartment building for bachelors. Instead, this looked like a house you'd raise a family in. At least from the outside. Cautiously I stepped out of the car, and made my way up to the front porch.

I hadn't even made it up the last stair before the front door swung open and Declan stood there vibrating. "I didn't think you'd come."

"Well, I decided I needed to start living my life for me, and not for anyone else." And to do that I needed answers. I stood in front of him waiting for something to happen and when we continued to stand out in the open for the entire world to see, I finally spoke. "Are we going to go inside, or did you want to do this out here?"

Immediately Declan moved to the side. He was shaking his head as I passed by him. "I lost my head there for a minute. I'm sorry. All I can think about when you're this close is how much I want to take you in my arms, and I have to fight myself."

Why my heart spasmed in my chest from those simple words, I had no idea. Nor did I know why I wrapped my arms around his middle and laid my head against his rapidly beating heart.

His arms went around me and for the first time since he left for Spain, I felt whole again. I breathed him in and never wanted to let go.

"Let's go sit down and talk." My fingers twitched at his sides making Declan lean back. He looked down at me with a furrowed brow. "That's what you wanted, right?"

"It is." I swallowed the emotion in my throat and let myself be vulnerable with him. "But this right here feels too good. I'm afraid I'll never get it back."

"I promise you that anytime you need it, I'll hold you in my arms." His thumb ghosted over the apple of my cheek. "Day or night. Rain or shine. Whenever you need it."

"Okay," I whispered as I took a step back. It shouldn't have been so hard to move away. If it was this difficult already, what was it going to be like when I left?

Taking my hand in his, Declan guided me into his living room. His house wasn't large, but it was nice. It was modern with an open floor plan. All the furniture was black with gray accents.

"When did you buy this house?" I asked as he stopped us in front of a large couch and sat down at one end.

"When I couldn't stand to live with my sister and her boyfriend for another minute longer." He chuckled. "Not that I planned to live with her forever. In fact, I never thought I'd live with her, but she forced me here when I was recovering, when she saw how I wasn't taking care of myself."

"What happened?" I asked the simplest yet hardest question.

One side of his mouth tipped up as he huffed out a breath through his nose. "I was so excited to play in Spain. You know that. When I signed that contract, I was on cloud nine." I nodded. I had been excited for him as well. Once I graduated, I had planned to go see him, and watched a few of his games. "And then it all ended, so abruptly by some fluke accident. Damn did it feel like Schwartz had razor blades on the bottom of his cleats in that pile up. I don't think you could even recreate what happened to me if you tried. It felt…" he swallowed harshly and clenched his hands at his sides. "Maybe it was never meant to be, but at the time it felt like my entire life ended that day. Not only was my calf muscle almost eviscerated, but I grew more and more depressed with each passing day until I wasn't functioning."

His fingers unfurled slowly before he reached out and took my hand in his. His long digits enveloped me just like the hug did earlier. It both calmed me and made me extremely nervous.

Brown eyes glassed over as he took in my features. "If I would have known…" His gaze dropped as his jaw started to pulse. "I would have done better for myself and for you. You have to believe me. I was too self-involved to realize how my actions might affect you."

Or I meant so little to him, I never crossed his mind.

"Don't think like that. I love you, Dani."

Had I spoken my thoughts out loud?

"Then why didn't you ever try to contact me?"

"There's no excuse good enough. All I can do is apologize and promise I'll never do it again. I never wanted to hurt you, and, in the end, I almost killed you." The glassiness that had shrouded his eyes finally slipped over his eye lid and ran down his cheek. He didn't bother to wipe it away. Declan wanted me to see how much his actions in the past hurt him.

I wanted so badly to tell him I loved him too, but the words were stuck in my throat. I could barely breathe as I took in the devastation written all over his face.

One second, I was sitting next to him on the couch and the next, I was straddling his thighs as I slammed my mouth down on his. I felt Declan's body come to life. Not only the huge cock he kept hidden behind his sweatpants either. With each swipe of our tongues, his body expanded as if I was breathing new life into him.

Strong arms engulfed me. I pressed my chest into his until I felt the frantic beat of his heart against my own. We broke apart panting, fighting for air only to crash back into each other. I couldn't get enough, and by the tightening of his hands that had moved to my hips and the low moan that escaped him, neither could Declan.

Wanting to be closer and consumed by the man underneath me, I did the one thing that nearly killed me. I extracted myself from his hold and lap.

"What are you doing?" He asked with a deep, husky rasp.

I didn't answer him with words. Instead, I showed him as I pulled my t-shirt over my head, and pushed my shorts down my legs. Declan's mouth hung open, and for the first time I felt self-conscious about my body in front of him. While I was getting better, my body didn't look the way it used to. My ribs still protruded, and my stomach was a little too sunken. No one wanted to have sex with skin and bones.

"I'm sorry," I muttered as I bent forward and started to grab my t-shirt off the ground.

Declan's warm hands clamped down on my arms and hauled me back in his lap. "What are you sorry for?"

With my eyes cast down at my naked frame, I tried to curl into myself, but he held me firm in his grasp. "I saw the way you looked at me. I'm not what I used to be."

"Do you feel how hard I am for you?" He pushed his hips up and ground his erection into my pussy. "How does that scream I don't want you? I'm dying to be inside of you. I'm beyond excited, but in shock."

"You are?" I peeked up at him to find hunger unlike anything I'd ever seen in his eyes.

"As long as you won't hate me in the morning."

I huffed out an amused breath. "I can't promise you that. I might very well hate myself tomorrow for what I'm about to do.

"And what's that?"

My answer was to lift my hips to gain access to his sweatpants to pull them down low enough for his cock to spring out. I didn't waste any time. If I thought too long about it, I would start to second guess myself and I didn't want that. I wanted to further our connection and see if Declan could make me feel like he did before.

Gripping his dick, I placed him at my entrance and slowly sank down until every inch of his glorious cock was inside of me. It felt like heaven. It had been too long.

"Fuck, I don't know how it's possible you're tighter now than you were—" His words were cut off when I rose up and then slammed down. With my hands on his broad shoulders, I rode him like a rodeo bull. The way he stretched me; I couldn't get enough. Declan dipped his head, taking my nipple into his mouth sucking and laving before moving onto the other. It was pure ecstasy.

Tipping my head back, I moaned as heat infused my body. I started to shake, unable to hold back for even a moment. And then Declan's thumb pressed into my clit and my world exploded. I screamed, arching my back and fell apart as Declan held me tightly. I slumped against him and every inch his skin touching mine buzzed like a live wire.

Declan growled as I felt warmth fill me. My eyes fluttered open to watch his face as he came. It was the most beautiful thing I ever saw. His eyes were half-lidded and the muscles in his neck strained as he pulsed inside of me.

His body went slack underneath mine as our sweat

slick bodies stuck together. I wasn't sure what would happen next. I shouldn't have had sex with him. I hadn't even heard him out.

Nothing good would come of this.

Slowly his eyes opened to reveal the Declan I knew before he left. His eyes were haunted by mistakes and pain. His hands started to roam over my back.

"I'll never let you go again."

FOURTEEN
DECLAN

I WOKE up to Dani's warm body draped over mine. In truth, I was surprised she was still here. While I didn't regret a single second of being buried deep inside of her last night, I knew she'd come to her senses and likely hate me even more this morning for taking advantage of her.

Still, I couldn't help but groan as I tried to move, and my dick rubbed along her inner thigh. I needed to get out of my bed as quickly as I could before I spread her pretty thighs and spent the day inside of her.

An alarm went off in the distance. It wasn't mine. Maybe it was Dani's. Why she had an alarm on the weekend, I couldn't imagine.

One eye cracked open and then she sat upright nearly taking my dick with her.

"Oh, God," she whispered, clutching her hand to her chest. "I'm so dead."

Wrapping my hand around her hip, I tried to pull her rigid body back down to mine, but Danica squirmed out of my hold. "What's going on?"

"I fell asleep here, and no one knows where I am," she answered as she jumped out of my bed. I blinked and she was gone. I could hear her rapid pace as she walked through the house. "Where the hell are my underwear?"

Jumping up to follow her, I found Dani on the floor with her ass high in the air. Her pretty pussy open and waiting for me. "Over by the plant." Picking them up, I held them out for her.

"Thank you," she whispered as she shimmied them on. "Oz has got to be losing his mind wondering where I am."

"Where did you tell him you were going?"

"I didn't really say. I let him assume I was going to be studying." She pulled her t-shirt over her head before she picked up her purse. "I don't know if I can even look. Maybe Lo kept him busy, but…"

Plucking her phone out of her hand, I bent down to see how many notifications she had waiting for her on her phone. It was then I noticed the time. It was only five o'clock in the morning. "Why do you have an alarm for so early on the weekend?"

Dani shuffled her bare feet. "So I can go run. It's peaceful this time of day."

"Dani," I sighed and rubbed the back of my neck. "You don't need to run *more*." I made the team run every practice. Probably more than I should, but it was making a difference with their endurance and speed. But now knowing this.

Ripping her phone from my hand, she hissed. "You don't know what I need."

"Maybe not, but I'd like to. Don't shut me out." I reached out only for her to slip through my fingers.

Her eyes trailed my body. "I have to go, and you should put on a pair of pants. You're too distracting." She eyed me hungrily for a moment before she stepped back. "Maybe they won't notice I never came home last night."

"And what are you going to do the other nights I drag you into my bed?" A bit presumptuous, but I wanted her to know I didn't plan on this being a one-time thing.

"I can't. Don't push me Declan. Last night was…"

"Amazing, fantastic. The best sex we've ever had." I supplied for her.

"Yes, all of those things, but I'm not sure I'm ready to be involved." Looking down at her feet, she continued. "I'm not the same person I was before. I'm damaged."

"And you think I'm not damaged?" I scoffed. "I'm beyond fucked up, but when I'm with you, I feel like…"

"Yourself."

"Yes." I moved toward her and wrapped my arms around her. "You feel it too. Don't fight yourself on something that makes us both happy."

Resting her cheek on my chest, one hand came up to run down my back. "And what if I told you running makes me equally happy?"

"I'd say you're a liar, but if running helps you that much then don't give it up. I'll — "

"Don't you dare change anything on account of me," she interrupted. Her blue eyes blazed as she stared me down. "I'm just like any of the other girls on the team."

"You are nothing like the other girls. First of all, you have more talent than all of them put together." It was still killing me that I couldn't go and dismember her previous coaches for ever making her feel less than.

Tilting her head to the side, her gaze trailed down my body before stopping at my dick. Unconsciously, she stepped forward, eyes hungry. If she kept looking at me like that, I was never going to let her leave. It was going to be next to impossible not to hide how my dick got hard around her at practice, but that was for another day. "And second?"

Not holding back, I spoke the words from my heart. "I love you, and not them."

"You shouldn't say that." She bit her bottom lip.

"Why? It's the truth, and I've told you before. I haven't stopped loving you. You may have stopped but—
"

"I haven't," she said so quietly I thought I might have imagined the words that came out of her mouth.

I reached out for her again and this time Dani let me take her soft hand in mine. "Then what's the problem?"

"I'm afraid of being hurt. What's going to happen to me this time when it doesn't work out between us? While I have the tools set in place from my therapy, I don't think they're enough for the heartache this will eventually cause."

"Things didn't go south between us, Dani. We didn't break up. I fucked up—royally—but I promise you I will never do that again. I've learned my lesson. I don't want to live in a world without you in it."

"We can't be together." She looked up at me with her big blue eyes grieve stricken. "It's against the rules. You should know that since you're the coach."

Fuck. I did know that, but it still didn't make it any easier.

"I'll quit." It was the simplest solution.

Dani's mouth hung open. She stepped forward until her hands rested above my heart. "I…" Her phone went off with another alarm. "Shit, I have to go." She patted me and stepped back. "Don't do anything stupid." Leaning down, she slipped on her shoes. "I don't know the answer. Hell, I don't know anything, but don't quit. We'll talk again."

It didn't escape me that Danica hadn't said she wanted to be with me. Perhaps she was trying to escape as last night's regret seeped in.

Grabbing her keys off the floor, she clutched them in her hand as if they were a lifeline. I didn't like that, but I wasn't going to say anything. I had to prove to Danica that she could trust me with her heart, but it would take some time.

"Text me when you get home, so I know you're okay."

Dani rolled her eyes and then headed to the front door. "Don't you start in on me too. I have enough watchdogs as it is. I can't handle you doing it too."

I moved forward only for her to take a step back. "It's only because we love you."

With her hand over her heart, Dani's eyes glassed over. "Maybe so, but I just want to live my life, and I can't do that with everyone hovering over me. For fucks sake, I lied to come here, and now I have to sneak back into my house. Which I won't be able to do if I don't get the fuck out of here." She shook her head, taking a step back. "I have to go." Tears brimmed on the edge of falling before she turned and walked out the door. My heart went right along with her. If she only knew she was the key to my happiness.

FOR THE LAST I had no idea how many hours, I'd been sitting on the couch waiting to hear back from Danica. I couldn't count how many times I picked up my phone ready to text Dani only to put down trying not to smother her.

When we were together before, our dynamic was so different. We were carefree college students. Well, as carefree as we could be as we tried to further our soccer careers. It killed me that mine was over and Dani's may never come to fruition. Dani was right. We weren't the same people as we were a couple of years ago. She made all the pain I went through fade away though. I only hoped I could do the same for her.

The doorbell rang making my head pop up.

Instantly I was on alert. While I loved my sister, I hoped like hell it wasn't her. She would know my head wasn't in the right place after one look at me.

Opening the door, I forced a smile on my face. Ready to play the part of the happy brother who finally had his life together. My face fell as my eyes land on a red, puffy eyed Dani standing at my door. One look at me and she started to cry.

Stepping forward, I took her in my arms and dragged her inside into my living room. "What happened?"

Dani shook her head as she cried into my chest. In less than a minute the front of my shirt was drenched with her tears. Unsure of what to do, I sat down on the couch and pulled her on my lap. All I could do was hold her and wait for her to calm down.

I had no idea what happened, but I did love that she came to me at the end of it.

Rubbing my hand up and down her back and running my fingers through her hair, I pressed my forehead to the top of her head. "Do you think you can talk about it now?"

"They all hate me," Dani sobbed out.

"What do you mean? Who hates you?"

Tilting her head up, she looked up at me with her big blue eyes that were spilling over with tears. "Oz, my best friend. Everyone at the house," she howled.

"No, they don't. Your brother loves you. More than anything."

"Not more than Lo, and she thinks I'm being stupid for spending any time with you outside of the field."

Damn that hurt.

"She's just worried you're going to get hurt, but if she knew my intentions, she wouldn't think that way."

Dani shook her head. "I can't let them run my life. I understand they just want to look out for me, but I can't live my life on lockdown." Her voice cracked. "They're all going to move away and live their lives after they graduate while I have two more years of school. What do they think will happen then?"

Tightening my hold on her, I kissed her forehead. "I don't know. If you show them how strong you are then they'll see they don't have anything to be worried about."

"Why are you so great? You weren't like this before," she cried.

I couldn't help but laugh. She was right though I wasn't like this, but I wasn't an asshole to her until I was. "Because I hadn't lost you before, but now I know what that feels like, and I never want that to happen again."

Her bottom lip stuck out before she wrapped her arms around my neck. "I don't know what I'm going to do."

Holding her close, I tried to push any ounce of calm and strength I had into her. "I'll help you anyway I can."

"I packed a bag and I left. I just couldn't take it anymore."

Rubbing her back, I asked. "What happened?"

Shaking her head no, she tipped her head back. "They

were all waiting for me. Staring at the front door. It was like I was late for curfew." Her eyes grew wide. "It was ridiculous."

"Yes, they should have called you if they were worried, but you should have told them you weren't coming home. They probably thought something horrible happened to you."

Her face cracked. A total look of devastation took over. "I know, and that's what they said." A sob ripped out of her. "I should have called Oz, but he would have blown a gasket."

"He loves you."

Her lips set into a thin line and her eyes narrowed. "Whose side are you on?"

"Yours." I cupped the nap of her neck and waited until her sad blue eyes met mine. "Always yours, but I know how much you love your brother, and he loves you just as much."

"He does. I know he does." Her chin quivered. "But I need to live my life for me and not him."

Taking her hand in mine, I brought it to my mouth and pressed it against my lips. "Did you tell him that?"

"Yeah, today I laid it all on the line," she nodded as tears streamed down her face.

Damn she was going to be pissed at me for telling her this, but I had to. "You should have told him how you were feeling before today. Did you ever tell him that you felt smothered?"

Dani looked down at the space between us for a long moment before she looked back up. "No."

"I hate to say it, but if you would have told him or any of them how you felt, things might be different."

"Of course, I know that now," she huffed. "But before you, I did nothing. All I've done is sit around the house, run, go to practice, and school."

I hated that for her. Dani used to be so lively, but her light had dimmed so much during our time apart. I wanted nothing more than to bring it back and help her shine.

"Okay, maybe give him today to cool off and realize how both of you feel, and then talk."

"They were all so mad at me, and I understand why. If any of them stayed out all night after insinuating they were studying, I'd be so worried." She closed her eyes and inhaled a deep breath. When she opened them again determination shone brightly. "The thing is, Lo was the one who said I was going out to study. She didn't know where I was going, but I thought she thought, I might be out for a hookup or something." She shrugged as if her words were no big deal. The thought of Dani with anyone else had me seeing red.

Dani patted my chest. "Down boy. I can feel the

steam coming off you already. While you don't own me because the only person who owns me is myself, I am not the type of girl who would go out for a random one-night stand."

Her words appeased the beast lurking deep inside of me. "The thought of another man's hands on you has me wanting to rip them from his body."

She laughed a sad little laugh. The corners of her pretty pink lips tipped up a slight amount. "I'd say don't go all caveman on me, but I can't say I feel any different thinking of you with another girl."

"You're the only one for me." I wasn't sure she could say the same for me though.

Tipping her head forward, she rested her forehead against mine. "Are we really going to do this? We'll have to lie and hide. That's no way to—"

"I'll do whatever I have to do. It's only temporary. It's not like it has to be forever." She started to close her eyes and shut me out. "Don't. Say whatever it is you need to say and look at me when you do it."

"It's not for this school year. I'll have two more years after this where I'll either stay in Willow Bay to finish up to be a physical therapist or I'll go somewhere else."

"If you leave, I'm following you." The words were out of my mouth before I could think. It didn't matter though they were one hundred percent the truth.

"And do what? Be a coach? We'll be in the same position."

"I don't have to be a coach." But if I wasn't, I had no idea what I'd do. I'd follow Dani to the ends of the earth if it meant I could stay with her. There was nothing that could stop me. I didn't give a shit if I was her coach or not.

"Don't talk like that. While I know you don't love it, you need a purpose."

"My sole purpose for being on this earth is to be with you. As long as I have you, I'll be happy and fulfilled."

In an instant the wetness was back in her eyes, but this time I knew it wasn't from being sad.

"Declan," she sighed out my name dreamily. Her mouth hovering over mine. "Don't make me regret this."

Before I could promise not to, her mouth was on mine. If I couldn't say it with words, I'd show her with my body.

FIFTEEN

DANICA

I ROSE UP and then down feeling every glorious inch of Declan's steel cock inside of me. I woke up needing him in a way I'd never felt before. The desperate hungry look in his eyes let me know he felt the same way.

"Fuck, you're beautiful like this." The blunt tips of his fingernails dug into the flesh at my hips. I hoped they would leave bruises to remind me this… whatever this was with Declan was real. He was the beautiful one. The way his brown eyes darkened as they took in every inch of me as I rode him. Tipping his head back, he groaned. "I'm not going to last long with you clenching around me like that."

Hell, neither was I. I was so close to the edge, I just needed a little more.

"Come for me, baby," he ordered, snaking his hand

around until his thumb found my aching clit and pressed hard.

White sparks of light filled my vision as my entire body shattered. I felt weightless for the first time since Declan left for Spain. I never felt this sense of ease while I ran or was out on the field. Collapsing on top of his chest, I closed my eyes as I tried to catch my breath. The sound of his rapidly beating heart soothed me. My heart squeezed in my chest before matching the rhythm of his.

Declan's hand ran up my back. "I could get used to waking up like this every morning."

While I loved waking up with Declan next to me, this wasn't how my life was supposed to be. My heart sped up for a different reason. What was I going to do about my brother? How did he not know how much pain I was in? Not once had he tried to call or message me since I left last night. I guess I deserved it since I didn't bother to tell him where I was the night before.

"Hey, stay in the present. Let me make us some breakfast burritos. We'll eat and then we can go talk to your brother."

"You're coming with me?" I guess I didn't hide the shock in my voice as well as I thought if the flare in Declan's nostrils was anything to go by.

"Unless you want me to stay here. I think if he knew

I never intended to hurt you, it might make him feel differently."

"It wasn't you that he has a problem with. I mean he does, but it's me he's angry with."

The hands on my back stilled and his body tensed. "Does he know where you were when you didn't come home the night before?"

I shook my head, wondering if this was going to be the beginning of the end. "I never even got the chance. I hardly got a word in edge wise."

"Maybe it would help if I apologized. I can explain that you wanted answers and I knew he didn't want me at his house again, so I asked you to come over. We fell asleep," he said nonchalantly.

I humorless laugh escaped my lips. "You make it sound so simple."

"We won't know until we try. I don't want there to be bad blood between you and your brother."

Neither did I. Never did I think anything, or anyone would come between us.

"I just want to live my life, and I know I fucked up. Big time, but living under their watchful eyes constantly, I'm going to flounder. Why can't they see it?"

"Listen," he pulled me closer. "Don't hate me for what I'm about to say, but how was your brother to know if you didn't tell him?"

"I know." I threw my hands in the air. I felt like we'd been having the same conversation on repeat. Everything was going around in circles, and I just wanted it to end."

"I know," he whispered. "Let's get cleaned up. We'll eat and then head over there. It's the only way to set things right."

While I liked Declan's optimism, I didn't think he realized how difficult it was going to be. Oz was stubborn. We had that in common. The only thing I saw in our future was us butting heads.

"What if he doesn't want to hear me out?"

Declan pulled back until I could see his face. His brows were knitted together and his mouth turned down at the corners. "Why wouldn't he? He loves you, Dani. You have to remember that. I'm sure he's hurt you lied to him, but he'll get over it."

"And if he doesn't?" That was what I was truly afraid of. What if I'd caused irreparable harm to my bond with Oz?

"Then you'll stay here until he gets his head out of his ass, but I don't see him being unwilling to listen to what you have to say or forgiving you. He just needs time."

I nodded because while every word coming out of Declan's mouth sounded true, there was something gnawing in the pit of my stomach.

"Alright, let's go." Declan slipped out from

underneath me and before I could even try to get out of bed myself, he pulled me along with him. I was sad when our shower ended up being a plain boring one. I was hoping for one more orgasm to help me forget what was happening in my life.

An hour later, we were pulling up in front of my house, or Oz's. Technically Fin and West's. It hurt that up until yesterday, it felt like mine. I'd barely gotten out of the car before the front door swung open and Fin was standing there in only a pair of athletic shorts and a scowl on his face.

"What's he doing here?" He growled. While it might have sounded threatening, it had warmth swirling through my chest. Fin cared about me, and I treasured that. He didn't let many close to him, and now I was one of those few. I only hoped it stayed that way.

"I'm here to apologize and to support Dani as she tries to talk to all of you," Declan answered, coming around the side of the car and clasping my hand in his.

Fin widened his stance in the frame of the door. "You're not welcome here."

"I know, but I'd like to change that. At the very least, let Dani speak and then I'll leave." His words sounded so confident. I didn't know how Declan did it when he knew they all hated him.

Holding his hand tighter, I stepped closer to the

house. Sadness filled me. I wanted this to be my home. I wasn't ready to lose my brother yet.

"Fine, come inside and say your piece. I can't promise anyone will listen."

Declan nodded; his head hung low. "Thanks."

Stepping in front of Declan to be the first inside, I found everyone standing in the living room. West stood next to the door with a worried expression creasing his usually happy face. Lo was wrapped around Oz's arm as if she was trying to hold him back. From what, I didn't know. It didn't matter. The sight broke me. Was I going to constantly make these mistakes and hurt the ones I cared about?

I started to turn around, unable to face them until I felt Declan at my back. He was here for me. He wouldn't leave or give up on me, no matter what. I believed he was sorry for cutting me out of his life before and he'd never do it again. I had to believe it because I couldn't face the reality of him breaking my heart again.

"You brought *him,* here?" Oz looked Declan up and down and found him wanting. "Dani what the hell is going on with you?" He deflated with a heavy sigh. "You're making one bad decision after the other."

"Don't talk about him like that. I made one bad decision and that was not telling you how I felt suffocated by the constant hovering."

"Did you know she felt like this was a jail?" Declan spoke up from behind me.

"You don't know anything," Oz barked out.

"I know exactly what she's told me. Do you really think all she wants to do is sit at home, go to practice, school and games? Don't be naive. She needs to live her life."

Oz pushed forward, ripping his arm from Lo's hold. Bypassing me, he went straight for Declan. "You," he pressed his finger into Declan's chest. "Have no idea what you're talking about. You didn't see her after you broke her heart. *You* didn't watch her almost wither away because she couldn't handle the thought of you being out of her life. *You* didn't see how those assholes brainwashed her into thinking she wasn't enough. *You* weren't there." Oz pressed further into Declan's space. His face was red. His body tense as he threw out my past like I wasn't even there. "I was. We all were. We picked up the pieces while you were god knows where."

"And I'll never be able to forgive myself for hurting your sister. I see her now, and I don't want to imagine how bad it got before she got help. What I do want is to be here to help her. To be another layer of support because I love your sister."

"If you loved her so much then why did you leave and never speak to her again?" Oz bit out.

"You know that's not true. We did speak after he left, but…"

Oz's angry blue eyes met mine. I couldn't remember a time where that look was ever directed at me. Tears pricked in the back of my eyes. "Semantics, Dani. I want this asshole to explain why he thought it was okay to hurt you."

Declan stepped forward, blocking me from Oz's view. "I didn't mean to hurt her. I wasn't thinking."

"Exactly," Oz shot out. "You weren't thinking. You dropped her like last week's garbage, and when she continued trying to seek you out, you blocked her. How am I supposed to believe you won't do that again?"

Declan's mouth went in a straight line as he stared at my brother. "I'll have to prove it to you. I was in a really bad place, and while I know that's no excuse, it's the truth. The physical and mental anguish I was going through prevented me from thinking about how my actions would hurt your sister. If she's willing to give me another shot, shouldn't you?"

"No, I'm here to protect my sister from assholes like you. If you haven't noticed she hasn't made the best decisions with her life since she met you."

Okay, hold up. I was not going to stand there and listen to my brother put me down like I was a toddler with impulse control issues.

"What I do and don't do with Declan is none of your concern." I pushed forward wanting all of his attention. "I don't know where this is going with him, but Declan makes me happy. Is that what you want, or do you want me to sit here in this house miserable, while the rest of you live your happy little lives only for you to then leave me once you all graduate?" I swept the room to find Lo and West staring at me with sad eyes. Fin looked ready to murder someone.

"If you want me out of your house just say it."

"How can you want to be with him? It wasn't that long ago when you were begging me to help you come up with a plan to take him down, and now you've fallen into his bed?" Fin scoffed as if he was disgusting with me. Maybe he was.

My stomach cramped at the thought of everyone I loved hating me. "You're one to talk. How much tormenting did you do to West because you didn't want to face the fact that you're gay for him?"

Fin's eyes turned an angry shade of black as his gaze drilled into me. "That's entirely different."

"Is it? How so? I didn't want to face the fact that Declan was back in my life as my coach after he ghosted me. I was hurt and angry the same as you, but look at you now, Fin. You're in love with one of the best guys I know, and happy. We all see it. Don't you want the same for me?"

Fin's dark brows pulled tighter. "Of course, I want you happy. We all do, but none of us can stand the thought of you getting hurt again and what it might do to you."

I understood that. There were no reassurances that my relationship with Declan would last. I didn't want to fall into that pit of despair and pick up my old habits. If I did, I might not make it out of the other side.

"What if I promise to talk to my therapist about my relationship with Declan? Explain to her my fears and yours." I didn't know what else to do to try and make this right for everyone.

"It's a start," Oz spoke up.

"I'll do whatever I can to make you trust me as long as I can live my life."

"And your life includes him?" Oz nodded to Declan.

"It does. I love him, and I believe him when he promised to never hurt me the way he did before."

One second Oz was standing a couple of feet front of me and the next, I was wrapped in his arms. "I can't watch you try to kill yourself again if he hurts you," he muttered as he pressed a kiss to the side of my head.

"I know what I'm doing."

"You need to talk to your therapist about this. I want to go with you to see what she has to say."

"Okay," I agreed easily. "Will you ever forgive me?"

One side of Oz's mouth tipped up. "You know I've already forgiven you. It's impossible for me to stay mad at you, but you can't hold back. Don't keep your feelings bottled up until the point of explosion like last night. If you had told me how you were feeling— "

"I know," I cut him off. All of this was my fault. "I didn't want to rock the boat, but I let it go too far. At first, I wasn't feeling it, but having to sneak out of my own home just to hear Declan out made me realize how I'd been feeling for far too long."

"This isn't a prison, Dani. You can come and go as you please, but I need to know where you are. Someone could have hurt you, and left you on the side of the road or worse. How was I to know you stayed at your ex's house?"

"And Declan explained that to me. I wasn't thinking. I also wasn't planning on staying the night. We fell asleep after being exhausted from hashing everything out. I didn't mean to scare you."

"But you did, and that's why I was so upset. Don't let it ever happen again. While I might not agree with your relationship with Declan, I won't want you to hide it. I don't want you to ever hide anything from me. Got it?"

"Deal." Wrapping my arms around his shoulders, I hugged my brother with all the love I had for him. I didn't know what I'd ever do without him, and I hoped I never found out.

"While I might have forgiven you, I'm not sure Fin will be as easy. He's been unbearable," Oz whispered so only I could hear him.

"And the rest?"

"You don't have to worry about them. Maybe take Fin out into the backyard and have a talk away from everyone else."

I had no idea what I could say to make Fin not angry or if he'd even listen, but I had to try. I couldn't live with the knowledge he was pissed at me. It wasn't healthy for either of us.

I tried to give Declan a reassuring look before I turned to Fin. "Can we talk out back?"

Fin's jaw ticked but he gave me one curt nod. "I'd love to hear what you have to say." He headed straight of the backyard with Charlie following at his heels.

"Good luck," Oz and West both said at the same time.

Declan took my hand in his. It was the strength I needed to face Fin. "Do you want me to come with you?"

"No, I have to do this on my own, but thanks." I

leaned into him. "Maybe you can make some headway with my brother while I talk to Fin.

"If you need me, I'm here." Leaning down, Declan kissed my forehead.

"Thanks." I took in a fortifying breath before I headed straight into the lion's den.

SIXTEEN

DANICA

MY HEART GALLOPED in my chest as I followed Finn's footsteps out to the backyard. He wasn't the easiest to begin with, and now I was on his shit list. How was I going to make him see what I'd done was wrong and Declan wasn't the enemy?

His back was too me as I stepped outside into the bright sunshine. He threw a ball across the yard for Charlie before his hands clenched at his sides. "Start talking."

"First off, I want to say I'm sorry about what I said in there about you and West. How you treated him before is and was not my business. I know you love him now and that's all that matters."

He whirled on me. Black eyes blazing and nostrils flaring. "Do you think I don't remember what an incredible asshole I was to him? I think about it every day. West never deserved the way I treated him," he seethed out.

"No, he didn't," I said quietly, wringing my hands together. "But he's forgiven you."

"How do you know?"

I couldn't help the mini scoff that escaped. How was he so dense sometimes? "Sorry," I held my hands up. "It's just that it's so obvious. West only looks at you with love. If he was holding onto any resentment you'd know."

Charlie came prancing back with the ball. The happiest dog on the planet. Fin took the ball from him and threw it again. I watched Charlie run after it for a moment before I turned back to Fin. "Talking about West is not why I came out here though."

"I assumed not. Say what you came to say," he grumbled, his body stiff.

"It wasn't right for me to ask you to come up with a plan to take Declan out at the knees. I only wanted to hurt him the way he hurt me, and saw no other way at the time. If I would have listened to him when he tried to explain what happened this probably wouldn't have happened."

"And what happened that made you magically forgive him? You wanted to end his career here, and instead you wound up in his bed."

I didn't like his words even though they were correct.

"I spilled out all of what happened to me when we were out of town for a game. I let it all fly out, and I saw the look on his face." Wrapping my arms around my middle, I looked over my shoulder to the back door. "He was devasted. Seeing that broke a tiny fissure of ice on my frozen heart away. I didn't forgive him right away though. I was still mad, but the man was persistent. He offered to answer any questions, and we talked." I shrugged. It sounded so simple now, but it was hell to get here.

"Are you sure it's not the orgasm talking?"

I rolled my eyes at him. "I'm sure. While he's very talented in bed, its more to do with the fact that I still love him. I have all this time and that's why I was so incredibly hurt."

"And how are you going to date or whatever is you plan on doing with your coach? Have you thought of the ramifications of what will happen if you're caught?"

I hadn't and the possibility of being found out was great. I shook my head. "I don't know how we're going to do this." My shoulders slumped. "What I do know is I want to be with him. I love Declan, and I probably always will. I owe us this shot to see if we can make it work."

Fin's arm brushed up against mine. "I want you happy, okay? What I don't want to see is your brother sick with worry. Hell, we're all worried. What happens if you get caught? Are you going to stop eating again?"

"I won't let that happen. I'll speak to my therapist about it, and if something bad happens I'll be prepared. But even if we don't last, I won't have anyone constantly whispering in my ear that I need to lose another couple of pounds. That all I need to do is hit the gym a little harder." I walked over to the table and chairs, and crumpled into the chair closest to me. "It's not like every time something bad happens my instinct is to not eat."

"No, but it is to run until you're utterly exhausted. That's not healthy either."

He was right. It wasn't.

Tilting my head up, I looked at Fin and waited until our gazes locked. "With each day, I'm getting better, but if the people I'm closest with don't believe in me I'm never going to be successful."

"We believe in you, but we're all scared."

"I'm scared too. I think that's part of life, and it's fine to be scared. If you're not, are you living to the utmost of your ability?"

"I like the way you think." He cracked a smile. "How much do you want to bet they are all at the windows trying to peak out at us to see if I kill you?"

"Uh, zero," I laughed. "One hundred percent there's

at least one person at the window." I took in a fresh breath of air. "Thank you for caring."

"Well, I don't like it, but it's not going to stop either." He spoke the last as he looked away to throw the ball again for Charlie.

"If it makes you feel any better, I care for you too. You're like a second brother to me."

He hummed before looking back at me. "But I'll never be the favorite since we don't have that special bond." He flashed his teeth letting me know, he wasn't bothered by the fact. It was true.

"True, but hopefully it's enough."

"I've always thought of you as the little sister I never had. Thank god, my parents didn't have any more children. Can you imagine the mess they'd be?" He shook his head.

"If they were anything like you, they'd be doing alright. You've done so much for yourself since you came to Willow Bay. You work so hard in all aspects of your life, and if your parents aren't proud of you, they should be."

"You know for a fact that my dad isn't proud of me. If he had his way, he'd ruin me."

I did know that. "That's because there is something seriously wrong with that man. While your mom can't express herself freely, she did make it possible for you to get your inheritance."

He nodded as he looked off at Charlie. "I can't imagine having to live in the football house with all of those guys. One year was plenty."

"What do you say we go inside and let them see you didn't kill me? I mean that is if we're good." I stumbled over my words. I didn't think my conversation with Fin would be this easy. West had definitely worked his wonders on Fin.

"We're fine, but don't come to me asking for a way to ruin his life if he breaks your heart again."

"I promise." I stood and moved closer to Fin. "Can I give you a hug?"

"Oh, for fucks sake. Why?"

"Because it will make me feel better about where we are, but if you don't want to, I can accept that."

"Fine, but make it quick," he grumbled with a deep frown marring his face.

It was the quickest hug known to man, but it still eased my soul. Fin wasn't the hugging type, but as his arm went around me to give me a quick squeeze only to be pulled away just was quickly, I smiled.

"Thank you."

"Don't mention it. Charlie," he called out before he started for the back door.

Fin might not have realized how much he'd changed, but he was like an entirely different man. If his parents wouldn't tell him they were proud of him, then I would.

Declan

It felt like forever and a day as I waited for Dani to come back inside. It didn't help that her brother was giving me the evil eye the entire time either. Finally, I broke the silence.

"Look, I get it. No one is ever going to be good enough for your sister. I have one myself, and she hid her relationship from me until they were caught."

"So, it runs in the family to hide who you're with?" He snarled.

"No," I shook my head sadly. I had no idea how Dani and I were supposed to work out when we couldn't let on that we were together. Hell, we were barely into the school year, and I couldn't imagine having to hide how badly I wanted to be by her side or touch her. Yet, I was going to have to figure it out one way or the other. I wouldn't let this ruin, Dani.

"Then what's the plan?" He asked after I was quiet for far too long.

"There isn't a plan in place. I offered to quit my job, but Dani wouldn't have anything to do with that. All I know is having your sister back in my life is making me happier than I've ever been." Clapping my hands together, I sat my elbows on my knees and leaned forward. "When I left for Spain, I never intended to hurt your sister, but when I got injured, I had an even bigger blow to my psyche. It's no excuse for hurting your sister, but if I had known…" My voice caught in my throat. How was I ever going to get over hurting the love of my life?

Oz cleared his throat as Lo gripped his hand like a lifeline. "I can see how much it hurts you, but if you ever hurt my sister again, I'll kill you. I don't care if it's even as insignificant as a hangnail."

"You know," Lo spoke up from his side. "I think the relationships that are so powerful that you can't stop them and are willing to do and go through any and everything are the ones that last." She stared into her boyfriend's eyes. "I think they're going to last."

At least one person believed in us. It was a start.

"I'd rather skin myself alive then ever hurt Dani."

"You better see that you do. She's had it hard enough without you breaking her heart again."

"I agree with you one hundred percent." Now for the next matter at hand. "Do you think Fin will let her continue to stay here?" While I didn't understand why he was angry with Dani, it was his house.

"While he doesn't act like it, he thinks of Dani as a sister." He looked to West and then back to me. "Fin's view on things can be a little skewed, but there is a heart in there somewhere deep down."

"I won't let him kick her out," West piped in.

"She worried about where to go once you all graduate. I'd happily have her at my place, but I'm not sure she's ready for that step."

Oz and West both nodded, but it was surprisingly West who spoke. "She can stay here for as long as she wants, but I think by the time we graduate—unless Dani wants some time by herself—she'd be ready to move in with you."

"I like how you all think you know what I want," Dani spoke from the hallway. "This is the type of shit I was talking about. Don't assume anything about me just like I don't assume anything about any of you. I had no idea if I'd be welcome into this house again, so I went straight to the source."

"And I say, she's always welcome here. I don't have any plans for this house. I may keep it as a place for college kids to rent once we're all gone, and by that, I mean Dani's extra two years. Don't worry about a place to stay. Ever," Fin said with a final disgruntled note. The man was definitely moody.

West stood and put his arm around Dani's shoulders, giving her a side hug. "We weren't trying to assume anything. I was only giving my opinion. I'm sorry."

"And I'm sorry for snapping. I'm kind of emotional today."

"Maybe it's your period," Fin mentioned with a frown.

"Doubtful, but thanks for keeping tabs of my menstrual cycle."

"Ugh," Fin gagged. "Let's not use that word again."

Dani cracked a smile. "I guess it's good you're into dudes otherwise, you'd never get a girlfriend."

"I'm into West. That's it." The statement was so simple, yet it meant so much.

Oz stood and patted his friend on the back. "Yes, we all know."

It was actually kind of sweet. I'd never had a dynamic like the one they had. They all cared deeply for each other that much was clear, but they also could give each other shit without blinking an eye. I wanted to be a part of this group if they'd have me. I guess I'd just have to prove myself.

Oz clapped his hands together and then rubbed them

with a wide grin on his face. "Since almost all of us are here, who's ready for a tournament?"

Dani nudged her brother with her shoulder. "Ford isn't here. He'll be so disappointed if he misses out."

"Then I'll call him and see if him and Xander want to play."

"Xander doesn't want to play," Dani said quietly.

Now that everyone seemed relaxed, I went to her side, taking her hand in mine. "What's this tournament you speak of?"

"Call of Duty. Have you ever played?"

"Hell, yeah, I've played. I'm so down with a tournament. Do you play?"

She was already shaking her head and laughing. "Not really. Me, Lo, and West suck. I think they just like playing with us because they know they'll win."

"Ford is down. They'll be here with lunch in about an hour." Oz yelled. His excitement filled the air.

Maybe just maybe I could be a part of this part of Dani's life too.

SEVENTEEN

DANICA

I WASN'T sure if I'd never noticed before or if it was a new development, but I swear every girl on the team was flirting with Declan. I wanted to claw their eyeballs out, and rip them to shreds, but instead, all I could do was stand there and grit my teeth.

"Danica," Declan barked out. "It's your turn. Snap to it."

Seriously? He thought he could just yell at me when all those girls fawned over him. He was lucky I didn't break his dick off.

Without even thinking, I kicked the ball with a hook, and it landed in the net. The other girls groaned. It wasn't my fault I could do this with my eyes closed.

I stayed as far away from Declan as I could, afraid I'd want to reach out and touch him. A week of this and I was close to losing my mind. How was this ever going to work? I couldn't keep acting like this or pretending like none of this bothered me.

A body brushed up behind me and before I could turn around, Declan's rough voice whispered in my ear. "What the hell is wrong with you?"

"I can't talk right now," I gritted out.

"You think I don't know that. Come to my house after practice and we can talk there." One finger drifted over the small of my back as he walked past me. I fought myself in not going after him like I had all week. I wanted to curl up in a ball and cry, or run until my legs gave out. I did neither. Instead, I tilted my chin up and pretended like nothing was wrong.

I wasn't sure how I was going to manage to be on a bus with him tomorrow for any length of time without wanting to touch him. I'd have to sit on the opposite end of the bus as him.

"What's wrong with you?" Staci snipped out.

"Nothing," I shot back as I slipped my feet in my flip flops.

"God, you're such a bitch."

"I don't care what you think. You only hate me because you'll never even be half as good as me." I smirked, and I knew it was a nasty smile.

"Miss Francisco, my office now," Declan demanded.

"Yes, Coach." I spun on my heels and headed directly to his office where he stood with a scowl on his face. I shoulder checked him as I stepped into his office.

Slamming the door, he turned around with his mouth in a thin line. "What the hell do you think you're doing?"

My eyes darted to the closed blinds, and I did what I wanted to do all afternoon. Stepping into Declan, I pushed him up against the door and swept my tongue through his shocked, open mouth.

Breaking his mouth from mine, Declan side stepped me. "Again, what the hell are you doing, Dani? We can't do this here."

"We can't do anything," I hissed.

His hands fell to his sides as he sighed heavily. "What's been going on with you?"

"Why are all those girls flirting with you?"

"I have no idea what you're talking about." Declan cocked his head to the side and raised one dark brow. "Are you jealous?"

"I'm not jealous," I snapped. "I'm pissed."

"I can see that, but we have to be careful, and you going into a jealous rage isn't that."

"I'm not jealous."

"So, you say, but your actions speak louder than

words." Sitting down in his chair behind his desk, he nodded toward the chair in front of him. "Sit."

I didn't like where this was going. "Am I in trouble?" I smirked.

"Talk to me, Dani. You've been acting off ever since we talked to your brother. I thought you'd feel freer, but instead you act like you're under lock and key. Is your brother giving you a hard time?"

"No, he's been great. Remorseful even for not asking me how I was feeling." Which in turn made me feel like shit. If I could have opened my mouth and talked to him instead of wallowing in my own pride things might have been different.

"That's good. If that's not it, then what's wrong?"

I was selfish. That was what was wrong.

"I can't touch you."

Leaning forward, he extended his hand out to me. "Not here, but there are plenty of other places you can."

"I don't like it," I pouted. I had no shame.

"Neither do I, but it's what we have to do. For now." He wiggled his fingers until I reach forward and clasped my hand in his. "Listen, I know this isn't easy, but we knew we'd have to hide our relationship."

"I did, but I never realized it would be this hard. I have no idea how Ford and Xander do it." They'd been hiding how they felt about each other for over a year, and they were growing strong.

"Maybe you should talk to them and see how they handle it."

Turning my head, I looked at the closed door and the blinds. He should have locked the door. "Why can't I even kiss you?"

"You want to tempt fate?"

"I don't think this is going to work," I muttered half to myself. I couldn't handle this kind of stress and anger for long, before I broke.

He was up and kneeling beside me before I could even blink. "Don't say shit like that. You think I don't want to kiss and touch you? Of course I do, but I also don't want the wrong person to find out about us and then have to deal with the consequences."

Looking down at him, I stared into eyes that made me want to take back the words that came out of my mouth next. "Aren't I worth whatever might happen?"

His jaw tightened as he shifted forward, and clutched my hand in his. "If you want me to open my office door and announce to all of those girls out there that you're the love of my life, I will. I'll shout it from the top of the stadium for everyone to hear, just say the word."

I deflated in my seat. He was making me feel like an impulsive child who was throwing a tantrum because I wasn't getting what I wanted. "Why are they flirting with you? Touching you?"

"Dani," he sighed, shaking his head. "They're not." My eyes narrowed on him. "Maybe a few have warmed up to me, but that's all. It's all innocent."

"How do you know? Are you in their heads? Are you asking them if they only like you as their coach as they reach out and touch you while giggling?"

"You know I don't." He closed his eyes and spoke. "Why don't you come over and stay at my place tonight. Although, it's probably not a good idea with us having to get up early to travel tomorrow."

I hadn't stayed another night since he'd brought me home after our first and only night together. In fact, I'd been more of a home body than usual. This was my fault. I should have gone to Declan, but I hadn't.

Standing, he leaned his hip against his desk and crossed his arms over his chest. "What are you thinking?"

"That I'm being ridiculous, and I should have come to your place before I exploded today."

Declan raised one brow. "I thought you had to study."

I did, but not that much.

"Are you regretting getting back together with me already?" He arms fell loosely to his sides.

"It's not that at all." I chewed on the inside of my

cheek. "I don't know how Oz will react when I tell him I'm going out and possibly not coming home."

"I can come to you," he offered easily.

"True, but I don't really want the entire house hearing us having sex in my room."

He hummed as one corner of his mouth tipped up. "That might be uncomfortable for everyone."

I rolled my eyes. "Trust me. The walls are paper thin. I spend ninety-nine percent of the time in my room with my headphones on, so I don't have to hear anyone having sex. It's my brother," I laughed. "And he's overprotective. In his head, he probably still thinks I'm a virgin."

A rich laugh boomed out of Declan. "Doubtful, but I'm sure he wishes it the same way I do about Roxy."

"I've known for too long that my brother wasn't a virgin. In fact, before Lo he was a manwhore. I held that against him for far too long, and I hate myself for it. He and Lo would have been together and happy, and maybe she wouldn't have been…" It still hurt to say that word out loud. Lo didn't deserve what happened to her. I was grateful for Oz, Fin, and West for taking her in when she was unable to leave our dorm room afraid of being attacked. That guilt on top of Declan leaving and my coaches was what sent me into my disorder. Once I was only focused on not eating and how to not be hungry, all of my other problems slipped away.

"Can you promise me something?"

"Of course."

He had no idea what he'd just promised.

"If you ever think I'm slipping, let my brother know."

The tips of his fingers trailed over the back of my hand. "Slipping how?"

"Not eating enough or running too much." I shrugged like it was no big deal even though it was. I could see myself falling back into old habits if I got into my head about Declan. I needed to remember he loved me, and he wouldn't cheat on me. He wouldn't shut me out again.

"I won't let that happen, and neither will your brother or his friends." He paused for a long second before he hooked his finger with mine. "Come to my house. I'll make dinner, we can watch a movie, and then I'll ravage your body all night long. How does that sound?"

"It sounds like heaven." I closed my eyes and whispered. "I wish I could kiss you right now."

"Me too. Every time you want to kiss me tap your lips with your index finger, and I'll know. I'll do the same."

"Kind of like our own private language." I smiled and tapped my lips.

"Exactly," he answered with a tap of his own lips.

"Now, get out of here before one of the other coaches comes in here to see what the hell is going on."

"You got it, Coach. I'll see you… soon." I tapped my mouth and then trailed my hands down my firm, flat stomach, and tapped between my legs.

Declan's eyes went hungry as he stood his ground. I couldn't wait for him to touch me when we were finally alone.

EIGHTEEN
DECLAN

I PACED my living room waiting for Dani to show up, tapping my fingers on my leg. It had been almost two hours since we parted ways, and I thought she'd be here by now.

I'd only just gotten Danica back into my life, and I already felt her slipping away.

Before when we were together, she wasn't the jealous type. I wasn't sure if it was possibly because she was insecure about her body or me. Either way, I needed to reassure Dani that I found her sexy, and I wasn't going anywhere.

The doorbell rang, and I nearly sprinted to the front door. Flinging the door open it took my eyes a few moments to adjust to the dark and the figure standing before me.

"Dani," I growled, grabbing her hand and pulling her inside for no one else to see.

She preened up at me. "Do you like what you see?"

"Like? I love." She was clad in only a black lace bra and thong with an open trench coat over it. "Please tell me no one else saw you like this."

She laughed and it was music to my ears. Unable to hold back, I moved forward, pressing her into the wall by the door. Ripping the coat off, I leaned forward and took one nipple roughly through the fabric of her bra.

She moaned my name as she threaded her fingers through my hair and held me to her.

One hand went to her other breast, tweaking her nipple with my fingers while my other hand pushed down my track pants and boxer briefs. The second my cock was free, her tiny hand gripped my shaft, and I nearly came undone.

Letting her nipple go with a pop, I grabbed her ass and lifted one leg to wrap around my hip. "I need you now."

"Yes," she answered breathlessly.

Pushing the fabric of her thong to the side, I ran my fingers through the slick folds of her pussy. "You're so ready for me."

"Fuck me, Declan. Own me," she begged, rubbing herself against my hand.

Crashing my mouth to hers, I tasted every inch of her mouth. Plundering her with my tongue the way I wanted to do with her pussy. As I ran my cock through her wetness, Dani angled her hips greedy to have me inside her. She wasn't the only impatient one. With one arch of my hips, I was deep inside her warmth. Her walls clamped down, and I waited for her to adjust to the fullness even though it felt like it might nearly kill me.

Breaking free, I sucked on her plump bottom lip, and nibbled along her jaw. My hands roamed up her sides, and massaged her breasts. When I left her relax, I finally moved.

"This is going to be fast and hard," I warned her. I gave her a moment to object, but when all she did was rise up and slam down on my cock, that was all the invitation I needed to fuck her with everything I had in me. With one arm wrapped around her back and the other under her leg, I pistoned into her like this would be the last time I'd ever have my cock inside of her.

With each upward thrust, her walls sucked me in deeper than the last. I nipped and sucked along her neck and collarbone, listening to her moan and chant my name as her fingernails scraped along my back. There was nothing better in life than this.

My balls tingled and I knew I was done for. Her pussy was too good. "I need you to come for me," I demanded as I angled her leg, opening her up for me and hitting her in just the right spot to have her come undone. Her body started to shake, and her walls nearly pushed me out she came so hard. I thrust once, twice, three times more before I bit down on the crook of her neck, and let loose inside of her for what felt like an eternity.

"Wow," Dani breathed heavily. "I think I need that every day."

"Agreed," I panted. Grabbing the other leg, I picked her up and carried her into my bedroom.

"I thought you were going to rip my lingerie off me," she laughed as I placed her on the bed.

"There was no time. My body took over and all I wanted was to be inside you." Running my hand up her thigh, I crawled onto the bed. "Next time, I'll take my time. Promise."

Closing her eyes, Dani sighed. "I could get used to this."

Pulling her until she was draped across me, I asked. "What's that?"

Tracing patterns along my ribs with her finger, she answered. "This soft, comfy bed, and you in it."

"I'd be more than happy to have you here." If I didn't think it was too soon and she'd say no, I'd ask her to move in.

"I'll come over more. I don't want to feel like I did this week." I rubbed my hand up and down her back, knowing there was more. "When I got home, I called my therapist and talked to her. It helped. A lot. If I would have talked to her or you earlier in the week, I don't think things would've gotten out of hand." Burying her face into the crook of my neck, she sighed. "It's hard you know."

No, I didn't know. I had no idea how she accomplished what she had. I wasn't sure if she'd always have a disorder or not. It didn't matter to me. I'd love her all the same.

"How is it hard?" I asked because I truly wanted to know.

"I don't want to disappoint anyone. While Oz now knows about us, he doesn't approve, so I don't want to run over here every night. I mean I do, but I don't want him thinking I'm making bad decisions."

My chest ached at the thought that I was a bad decision, but I didn't say anything. Maybe Dani would be better off without me in her life.

"But I know if I keep going like I did this week it's only going to hurt you and me, and I don't want that. I have to talk to Oz and make him understand."

"I think that would be a good idea." Inhaling a deep breath, I held it in for as long as I could and then spoke words I never wanted to come out of my mouth again. "Is it too soon for you to be in a relationship?"

"My therapist thinks I should be fine as long as I don't hold in what I'm feeling, and that's what I'm working on." Raising her head, she looked up at me. "I unloaded on you today, and that wasn't fair to you and I'm sorry." Her blue eyes scanned my face quickly before she laid back down.

Kissing the top of her head, I tightened my hold on her. "You don't have to be sorry. Just know that I'm always here for you to talk to even if it's something you think I won't like."

"You've changed."

"Is it a bad thing?"

"No. While I liked you before, this Declan Hart is amazing. It makes me love you more. Before I don't think I would have been able to open up to you like this."

While I knew I'd changed over the last year, the thought that Dani wouldn't have been able to talk to me has me thankful for my transformation. I knew in some ways I was harder, but when it involved the blonde splayed out on top of me, I was as soft as a teddy bear. If I hadn't lost her once before I probably would be the same asshole. We'd both changed so much since we were last together.

"I guess I'm thankful for my crippling injury."

Dani's hand ran up my arm and along my torso in feather light touches. "I wish you hadn't gone through that. I know how much it hurts to lose your dream."

"Hey," I lifted her chin with one finger until she was looking up at me. "Your dream isn't over yet. Don't give up. I'm doing everything I can to get you noticed."

Her eyes turned glassy as she stared at me. "I don't know what I did to deserve you, but I'd do it all again. A thousand times." Leaning down, she pressed her lips to the skin over my heart. "I love you."

Damn did it feel good to hear those three simple words come out of her mouth. It would never get old even if I lived to be a hundred years old.

"I love you too. Now let me show you just how much." Flipping her onto her back, I hovered over a smiling Dani. She was so damn beautiful. I would do everything in my power to always have her looking exactly as she was now. Sated, happy, and in love.

WRINGING MY HANDS TOGETHER, I stood in front of my brother and Lo. They were cuddled up on the couch watching a movie they'd seen together a thousand times. Still, I hated to interrupt them, but it was the first time Fin and West had been out of the house when I was there in I couldn't remember how long. I had to strike while I could.

"Can I talk to you?" My words were quiet and unsure, and I hated myself for being weak.

Oz sat up and immediately turned off the TV. "Sure. What's up, sis?" His blue gaze swept over me before his brows pulled together. "Is everything okay?"

"Yes. Kind of," I amended. I fought with myself to not fidget on the spot.

Lo tilted her head to the side reading me before she

reached out her hand. "Come over here and sit down. Whatever it is, we'll figure it out. We all love each other."

She was right. I sometimes forgot. In some ways it felt as if I'd lost Lo to my brother. She spent most of her free time with him, but I also understood why. She loved my brother more than anything. The same way I love Declan. That's why I was doing this.

Moving to be closer, I sat on the table in front of them. There wasn't much room on the couch for all three of us, and I needed some space. They each took one of my hands and squeezed. Oz's was big and rough while Lo's was as soft as silk. They were so different, but fit together perfectly.

"I've been struggling."

Oz's brows shot up. "What? When?" He stumbled out.

"Since our fight," I admitted, looking down at my hand in his.

He looked to Lo and then back at me. "I don't understand."

Of course, he didn't. He was so unapologetically in love with my best friend. Once they finally got together there was no stopping them. They didn't care if I approved or not.

Blowing out a breath, I sat up straighter. I needed to get this off my chest, so that I could live the life I wanted to live. It wasn't like I was off smoking meth or anything like that.

"I've been making up excuses not to see Declan because—"

"What did he do to you?" He growled out. His body going ridged.

"Nothing," I laughed. "He's been nothing short of amazing. I promise. It's all me."

"Explain," my brother demanded.

"I'm trying, but you keep interrupting me. Just let me get this out. It's hard enough as it is." When Oz only nodded, I continued even though I was scared to do so. Lo reached her free hand over to clasp onto Oz's forearm. "I want to spend time with Declan, but I also don't want to disappoint you." His brows furrowed together, and I knew I needed to explain myself better. "I know you don't want me with Declan, so when I go to his house, I feel like I'm letting you down. I don't want to care what you think, but I do because you're my twin brother and I love you. So damn much, and it kills me to know you're thinking badly of me and that I'm making a mistake while I'm gone."

I blew out a heavy breath, and wished Declan was here. He'd be so proud of me.

"Can I speak now?" He asked after several beats of silence.

"Yes, please." I needed to know what he thought.

"While I don't love you with Declan it's not for the reasons you think. Well, maybe some of them. I am worried he's going to hurt you again, and this time we won't be able to save you."

"That's why I've been talking to my therapist more. While I don't think Declan will purposely hurt me, I want to be prepared in case it does happen."

"Okay, good." He nodded. "I do believe he loves you, and doesn't want to hurt you. And while that might be true, I worry about what will happen if you're caught together. Do you really want to hide your relationship with him until the school year is over or after that?"

I laughed at that. "Of course, I don't, but I have no other choice. He offered to quit his job, but I wouldn't let him. He lost his ability to play, so I can't take away this."

"It's only going to end in disaster if you're found out."

"I know, and it's already driving me crazy that I can't touch him during practice."

Oz's face scrunched up. "I don't need to know about that."

"Just like I don't need to know how many times a day you have sex with Lo, and yet I do." I pointed out. "I'm going to talk to Ford and Xander, and see how they're doing it." I hung my head. "While I don't like hiding my relationship, I'd rather have it this way than no way at all.

I need him in my life. He makes me so unbelievably happy. Don't you want that for me?"

"Of course, I do." Oz scooted forward on the couch. "We all do. I just don't want to see you get hurt, but I promise you when you walk out the door, I'm not disappointed in you. I'm proud of how strong you are, and how much you've accomplished in your life. Don't hold back seeing Declan because of me. I don't want you miserable. Just come and talk to me like you did today."

Launching myself into him, I hugged my brother. He was always so understanding. Why did I wait so long?

"Thank you," I cried onto his shoulder. "I'm working on opening up and not bottling everything inside. I love you."

"I love you too," he hugged me back fiercely. "Your boyfriend doesn't have to be a stranger. Have him come over for dinner and spend time with us, so we can get to know him more. Maybe then I won't hate him so much." I pulled back and he gave me wink. "Seriously though, don't be a stranger. I love you. You can always talk to me."

"Ditto." I wiped at the tears that were streaking down my cheeks. "I love you both." Pushing back, I braced my hands behind my back. "Now, if you don't mind. I'm going to go see my boyfriend."

DECLAN'S warm hand ran up my back and tangled in my hair. "How'd it go?"

"Like I never had anything to worry about. Which I knew I didn't. I only needed open up about the way I was feeling, so he'd know." I hated that I'd become this closed off person who couldn't talk to the people that mattered most to me. It was all in my head and I needed to get it set straight.

With both hands on his shoulders, I adjusted myself to straddle his muscular thighs. "I have a favor to ask of you."

"Anything." He didn't even pause, and I knew Declan would give me everything I ever asked for.

"Come with me to Ford and Xander's house for dinner tonight."

"That was fast." He smiled, running his thumb along the curve of my jaw.

"I know. I think they know I'm having a crisis and accommodated my request. Well, I asked if I could just talk to them, and Ford offered dinner. And I can't turn down Ford's cooking."

"I'd be more than happy to escort you to dinner." He looked at the watch on his wrist. "How long do we have until we have to be there?"

If the growing bulge in Declan's sweatpants was any indicator, I had an idea where this was going. "He said seven o'clock." I swiveled my hips. "I think we have enough time to…" I smirked and slid off his lap, and onto the floor. Before I could move, Declan was already pulling his pants down. His thick, long cock sprang free, bobbing enticingly in front of me. My mouth watered at the sight of it.

"Fucking hell, Dani. You can't look at me like that." He ran the tip of his mushroomed head along my bottom lip. I stuck out the tip of my tongue to taste him. "I'm seconds away from shoving my cock down your throat and fucking your mouth."

Running my hands up his thighs, my lips tipped up. "Promises, promises." I licked along his slit and tasted his salty precum before I opened my mouth and sucked on the tip.

"Fucking hell, your mouth is magic." He arched his hips slightly letting me know he needed more.

Opening my jaw, I slowly took each inch until he hit the back of my throat. Swallowing him down, I held there for a moment before I slowly bobbed up and down, running my tongue along the bottom vain. I could feel him swelling more and more with each stroke.

His fingers threaded through my hair and held it back from my face. "God you're beautiful like this," he groaned. His dark eyes were fixated on my mouth stretched around his cock.

My clit ached to be touched, but this was all about Declan. I wanted to show him how much he meant to me. Rubbing my thighs together to alleviate the pressure, I focused all my attention on him.

Massaging his balls with one hand, I gripped his cock with the other as I quickened my pace knowing he was close, going by the trembling in his legs. Sucking on the tip, I ran my tongue along the bottom causing his hips to spasm.

"Fuck, Dani, I'm going to come." His face was one of awe. I loved that I could make him look like that.

With him still inside my mouth, I smiled as best I could and doubled my efforts. Swallowing his entire length one last time, I felt the tip slide down my throat before he unloaded down my throat with a shout. His grip on my hair tightened as he slowly fucked my mouth as stream after stream of his cum filled my mouth for me to swallow down.

Wiping my mouth, I looked up at him from between his legs. He was leaned back on his couch with his eyes half-mast as he looked down at me with soft brown eyes. Releasing my hair, he ran his hand up my neck and along my jaw. His thumb caressed my cheek.

"I need a moment to recover, and then I'm going to make you come so fucking hard you'll see stars." Reaching down, he picked me up and cradled me in his arms, nuzzling his face into my neck. Closing my eyes, I relaxed into his arms. I never wanted to leave his warm embrace. After several long moments, he spoke quietly, reverently. "I love you."

"I love you too." It felt so good to say those words, to feel his love and know that I was worthy of him when I never thought I'd feel that way again.

EVEN THOUGH I said I'd go with Dani to see her friend, I was nervous. Here we were going to try and figure out how to hide our relationship and be happy. Who would have thought I'd ever be here?

The front door opened to a tall man with dark hair that swept over one eye. I'd seen him once before when Dani invited me to their Thanksgiving. He must have been Ford.

"I'm glad you're here," he smiled, pulling Dani into a hug.

"Me too. At first, I felt bad about taking your room." She pulled back and grinning up at Ford. "Now, I see why you weren't too sad to leave the house. Well, that and your hot boyfriend."

A smile broke out on his face. "He is hot, isn't he?"

"Are you talking about me?" A smooth voice asked from deeper into the house.

"No," Ford yelled back at the same time Dani responded back with a yes.

Dani giggled, grabbing my hand. "You remember Declan, right?"

"Yeah, how's it going man?" His tone wasn't as bright as when he greeted Dani, but that was okay. Eventually he'd learn to like me or not.

"Good. Thanks for having us." Damn this was awkward. Would they all hate me forever?

"Yeah, it's a bit of an unconventional dinner, but we're happy to help. Come inside."

"Thanks." Placing my hand on the small of Dani's back, I followed them inside.

"It's even nicer inside," Dani exclaimed, nudging Ford's shoulder.

"I never said I lived in a dump, and I've invited you over for dinner before."

"I know," she said quietly. "I'm sorry for turning you down until now. It's different when you cook for all of us."

"I love cooking." He looked down at her knowingly. "I didn't ask you for any other reason."

Damn, they had all been taking care of Danica while

I was away. What would have happened if they hadn't been in her life?

Wrapping my hand around Dani's hip, I pulled her into me.

Her brows pulled together, and her nose scrunched up in the cutest way. "What's going on? We just got here," she whispered the last part.

"I know. It's not *that*." I could keep my dick in my pants for a few hours. "I just want to say I'm glad you have them."

"Who's them?" She nodded her head toward the two men in the kitchen.

"All of your friends, and your brother. They took care of you when I wasn't there."

Her mouth opened in a soft 'O', and her hands traveled from my waist to my chest to rest right above my heart. "I have no doubt that if you would have known, you would have been there."

I sure as hell hoped so.

"Thank you for coming with me. I don't know why I'm nervous, but I am."

"Will you look at these two? They're so in love." Ford said as he walked away to the other room.

Dani's face broke out into a large smile as she giggled. "Oh, my god."

Dipping down, I pressed my lips to hers. It felt good

to be able to do that out in public. I mean it wasn't public, but it wasn't only inside my house. Pulling back, I cupped her cheek. "We should probably get in there."

"Yeah. Is it bad that I kind of don't want to? All I want to do is go back to your house and get in your bed."

I nipped at her bottom lip. "While I like that idea, let's do it after we have dinner that your friend so kindly cooked for us."

"If you two lovebirds are done, dinner is ready." Ford called out with amusement laced in his tone.

This time it was Dani who mentioned we should go. "We're not being very good guests. They'll probably never have us over again."

"I think we can turn it around, and they'll be asking for us to come over every week."

"You're on," she laughed. With my hand in hers, Dani pulled me along behind her as she walked us into the kitchen. "I'm sorry, we…"

"It's all right." A tall dark-skinned man said as he placed a bowl on the table. "Sit down and we'll talk."

"That's Xander, in case you didn't know." Dani pointed out.

"I'm the worst host. I should have come to the door with Ford, but I didn't want to overwhelm you." With a blinding smile, he walked toward me with his hand out. "I'm Xander. I'm a professor at the university."

"I'm Declan, and the girls' soccer coach."

Xander chuckled. "We already have something in common."

"And here I thought tonight was going to be awkward." And it most definitely was, but I was going to do this for Danica. I'd do anything for her.

He sat down at the head of the table and Ford sat at the other end. "If we can't laugh about it, what are we going to do?"

He was right.

Pulling out a chair, I waited for Dani to sit before I sat across from her.

"Why don't you pull out my chair?" Xander asked.

Ford only stared at him from across the table before he picked up a plate and started forking out a piece of fish.

"This all smells amazing. Dani's been telling me what a wonderful chef you are."

"Thanks," he muttered, his eyes going to Xander.

"He's way too humble about his cooking. Wait until you taste it. His food will blow your mind."

"And now you know why I need to be humble. Everyone else blows my food up way too much. Anyway, we're not here to talk about my food, we're here to talk about the two of you."

"Not just us, but you two," Dani said around a bite of food.

"Yes, let's get down to the nitty gritty on how your boyfriend and I are doing unethical things concerning our jobs," Xander chuckled, lightening the mood.

I barked out a laugh. "In my defense, Dani and I were together before I was her coach."

"So, you just can't help yourself?" He chuckled.

Dani's foot ran along my calf. "Not a chance."

"And what about you?" Dani shot out; her brows pulled together.

It was sweet she was coming to my rescue, but I didn't need it. I was a big boy.

I wasn't a foodie, so I had no idea what kind of fish I was about to eat. I didn't exactly love fish, but I was going to grin and bear it. The second the bite hit my tongue; I couldn't help but moan.

"Damn, this is good. I don't even like fish, but I'd eat this every day." I pointed to my plate.

Ford nodded and looked around the room. I had a feeling he didn't love all the attention he got from his cooking. When he changed the subject, I knew I'd keep my praise to a minimum.

"If it wasn't for the blackmail, I'm not sure where we'd be."

I coughed almost choking on my food. "Blackmail?"

Ford's brows rose up. "At least, you don't have that going for you. It was the only way he'd still see me after he found out I was a student."

Clearing my throat after nearly choking, I spoke. "Wow, your dynamic is far more serious than I knew."

"Yeah, we're who you should emulate," Xander laughed.

We all laughed with him.

"How do you do it?" Dani muttered. "Half the time, I can barely function. I can't touch him or barely talk to him, while I watch all these girls throw themselves at him."

"Okay, just for the record, no one is throwing themselves at me." Putting my fork down, I looked at each person around the table. "Yes, I have to talk to them. It's my job, but I'm not interested in anyone but Dani."

"They're so in love." Xander said in the most nonchalant way ever. I liked that they could see how much I loved Dani. Their house felt like a safe place unlike the rest of the world

"It's cute." Ford didn't sound like he thought so, but that was okay. Since I wasn't exactly swooning over him and Xander, I understood.

"Just like how much you love Xander," Dani quipped.

"Now can we get to the matter at hand, how do you guys do it?"

"Well, it's a little different between two men and a man and a woman," Ford started until Dani slapped his shoulder.

"I understand the dynamics of your sex life just fine. Tell me how you don't explode every time you're out in public and can't even hold hands."

I wished the seating arrangements were different, so I could hold her hand. All I could do was bracket her feet with mine.

Ford cleared his throat and sat up straighter in his chair. "It's not as difficult for us because our worlds don't clash much outside of here. It has to be extremely hard to be around each other so much of the time and act professional."

"It is so hard," Dani whispered before taking a long drink of her water.

"With it only being the beginning of October, you have a long way until the end of the school year. When does soccer end?"

"That's the thing. The fall season ends in November, but then we pick back up for the spring in February, and that lasts until the end of the school year," I informed them. It wasn't like we would only have to hide our relationship until November and then we'd be free.

"Well, damn that sucks." Ford leaned forward with his elbows on the table and steepled his fingers in front of his face. "You have to decide what you want. You either have to break up because you can't take how hiding your relationship makes you feel, or you suck it up and keep going as you are."

"Wow, that's not helpful at all," Danica deadpanned.

Ford shrugged before he went back to eating. "That's the way it is. Do you think I like hiding Xander? No, I don't, but it's better than the alternative of people finding out and him getting fired."

"Who are you hiding from? You don't have any other friends besides my brother, Fin, and West," Dani shot out.

Ford flinched for only a second. If I hadn't been looking at him, I wouldn't have caught it. Still Dani had wounded him.

"And do you have any other friends outside that house? No, I don't think so. Still, I have other people I talk to in my culinary classes. I had to choose whether I would say I was single, or if I would say I'm with someone."

"I hope it was the latter." Xander's voice was missing the happy tone from earlier and now riddled with darkness.

"Yes," Ford rolled his eyes. "The only problem with

that is I had to make up a name, and he can never meet anyone at school. It's a double edge sword, but it's worth it."

At least he thought so.

"The same goes for me, but I had to tell the women I work with I have a boyfriend which I'm sure they all think I'm making up, because they were constantly trying to set me up."

"So, it sucks all the way around. Gotcha," Dani laughed dryly.

Xander leaned over and placed his hand over hers. "Did you think you'd come over here and we'd tell you how to magically be able to do what you want? There's no spell that will give you what you want unfortunately." He cleared his throat and looked around the table nervously. "Have you ever thought you might be jumping into a relationship too quickly?"

"Yes," she mumbled quietly. "But I've talked to my therapist, and she thinks if I communicate how I'm feeling when it's happening, I'll be fine. Plus, we've added an extra session in that's dedicated what happens *if* something happens, so I'll be able to handle it."

While I couldn't predict the future, I didn't like Dani thinking there was an expiration date on us. She was who I saw walking down the aisle to me, and growing round with my children. If we broke up, I would need therapy to get through it this time.

"We're not breaking up," I growled, a little too loudly going by how fast everyone's head turned in my direction. "I don't see any circumstance that would end us unless you get tired of me," I amended, my tone quieter this time around.

Dani's eyes lit up as she flashed me a bright smile. "I can't decide if I want to continue eating this amazing food, or if we should leave so I can fuck you."

My mouth full of risotto nearly clogged my throat at her words. I sputtered a few times before any words came out. "While I like what you just said, it would be impolite for us to leave after Ford slaved over the stove to make us probably the best meal I've ever eaten."

Dani tilted her head to the side. "Are you choosing food over sex with me?"

"That's not what he was saying at all," Ford laughed. He looked to me. "Thank you for the compliment. I appreciate it. It looks like you'll be around for a while," he smirked. "And you'll get to eat more of my food."

"I hope so." Putting my fork down, I braced my hands on the table. "So, you won't mind if we leave you with our half-eaten plates and all these dirty dishes?"

Dani threw her napkin on the table and pushed her chair back as she stared at Ford.

"I don't mind at all. It happens more often than you think." Ford smirked over at Xander who was shaking his head with a smirk of his own.

"Great. I promise we'll do this again. Soon." Taking my hand in hers, Dani nearly hauled me out of my seat as she waved goodbye.

It was me who was close to picking her up and sprinting to the car to get back to my place. I couldn't wait to sink inside her sweet heat.

WE'D GROWN COMPLACENT. Declan tried to keep his distance, but I knew he was afraid I was going to lose my shit, so he let me stay in his room on most of our away games. Now we were paying the price.

"Coach," someone banged on the hotel room door again. "Nicole is throwing up and won't stop." The banging continued as we looked at each other in the dimly lit room. The moon lit up the bed and Declan's face that was full fear.

"Coach," she screeched from outside the door.

"Coming," he barked out hoarsely. "Get dressed," he whispered-yelled.

Scrambling off the bed, I slipped on my tank top and shorts as Declan pulled on a pair of sweatpants. "You need a shirt," I hissed as he walked to the door.

Declan waved me off before he opened the door. "Chloe, what's going on?"

"She's throwing up and won't stop." Chloe sounded frantic. I guess I would be too if the person I shared a room with was throwing up continuously. Luckily for me, I never had a roommate.

"Okay," he yawned and stretched. "Let's go see how she's doing." Looking back into the room, he waved me away like I was going to come along with him. I could hear the commotion of a group of girls out in the hall. How was I ever getting out of his room?

Sitting on the edge of the bed, my knee bounced as I listened to what sounded like half the girls on my team talk about partying and their boyfriends. I was a little jealous that I couldn't be out there and share, even though I wouldn't share if I wasn't dating our coach.

We couldn't keep doing this. We were going to get caught, and Declan was going to lose his job. At first, I wasn't sure if he liked his job, but now I could see it. I didn't want to take the last remaining piece of the sport he loved away from him.

I wished I could call him and see what was going on, but I couldn't risk it. The last month had been perfect. Most nights I spent at Declan's house, but occasionally he came to our house, ate dinner with us, and spent the night. Oz and Fin weren't giving Declan the evil eye anymore. So, why did I feel so helpless all of a sudden?

Once the commotion died down in the hall, and I knew it was time for me to leave and make it back to my room before something more happened. Sliding my feet into my tennis shoes, I crept to the door like someone would be able to hear me inside.

Normally we had connecting rooms. Not that anyone knew, but this hotel didn't offer that option. I was only two doors down, but it seemed like a mile as I cracked open the door and peeked outside. I was certain there was someone lurking just outside to catch me, but there was no one. They'd all gone back to their rooms or to Nicole's. I had no idea, and I didn't care. All I wanted was for to get to my room undetected. Once inside, I closed and locked my door behind me, unsure if I wanted Declan to come to me when he was finished or not.

Slipping under the covers, I laid on my back looking up at the ceiling. I wasn't sure if I'd fall back asleep. I was too used to Declan's arms around me and the warmth of his body next to mine. My hotel bed was cold and hard. Nothing like the mattress at his place.

I had no idea how long I stared at the ceiling, but eventually I fell asleep. When I woke up from my alarm, I was still alone as was to be expected, and more tired than when I fell asleep. It was close to time to leave, so I packed up what little I had, and headed to the bus. I couldn't wait to get home. All I wanted to do was curl up on the couch and watch a movie with my best friend. I missed her and the simplicity of our friendship.

There were only a few of my teammates on the bus when I stepped inside. I didn't pay close attention to who was on the bus as I dropped down in the first open seat. Slipping in my earbuds, I pulled up one of my playlists, and turned it on before leaning my head against the window hoping sleep would find me soon. It was only a four-hour bus ride, but I'd take all the sleep I could get.

Feeling the vibration of footsteps on the bus, I opened my eyes to see most of the girls waiting to get on. Nicole's face was green as she leaned against Chloe. She looked like death warmed over. I was ninety-nine percent positive it wasn't from being sick and from drinking far too much. If it had been the former, I would have felt sorry for her. Instead, all I felt was deep seated animosity for ending my night with Declan and all the thoughts swirling in my head. Don't get me wrong, I didn't like the majority of my team. The only ones who gave me the time of day were the new girls who joined the team. It didn't bother me though. I couldn't afford to become close to any of them. If I did, all I could do was lie to them. I wasn't going to tell them about my eating disorder or my boyfriend. The only thing we could talk about was school and soccer, and that didn't make for a friendship. At least not in my book.

Closing my eyes, I didn't open them until I felt my phone buzzing in my lap. I already knew who it was from. Unlocking my screen, I stared down at the message.

DECLAN: Why'd you leave last night?

I WASN'T sure if I should answer him now or not. Without knowing where he was sitting, I didn't want to take the chance that he could see me avoid his message either. Damn it, I didn't want to do this here *or* now.

Dani: Why do you think?
I can't do this.

TURNING my phone on do not disturb which I should have done when I got on the bus, I turned up my music and rested my head against the glass. Even as the scenery passed me by, I saw nothing. All I could think about was

Declan. The feel of his eyes on me was profound, but I never looked back. I knew I'd see the worry in his eyes, and it would eat away at me.

I was never more thankful for one of our bus rides to be over than I was that day. I was up and out of my seat first and hitting the pavement quicker than anyone else. Half of them were still asleep, but I knew Declan wasn't. I hustled over to where Oz and Lo were waiting for me in Oz's car.

"Hey, sis. Where's the fire?" Oz laughed as he took my bag from me and put it in the trunk.

"The bus reeks of desperation. Let's get out of here."

"Alrighty then. Are you sure you don't want to say goodbye to your boyfriend?" Oz asked as he slid behind the wheel.

Lo placed her hand on his arm as she watched me with knowing eyes. "Leave her be. You know she can't properly say goodbye in front of everyone."

Thank god for Lo. If it wasn't for her, I probably would have bit off my brother's head when all I wanted to do was go home and cry into my pillow.

"Is everything okay between the two of you?" My brother asked softly. He was concerned probably because I was being moody.

I lifted a shoulder, but didn't speak. There was

something about saying the words out loud that felt wrong and permanent.

"What do you say we have a girl's day? We haven't had one of those in a while. We could get out of Willow Bay, grab some lunch, get our nails done, and do a little shopping."

While I knew it wasn't healthy to run away from my problems, I was in desperate need of some girl time with my bestie.

"That would be amazing. I need to take a shower and get the stench of the bus off me, but then I'd be ready to go."

Out of the corner of my eye, I saw Oz give Lo a look. I wasn't sure what it was for, and I didn't care. He could give her up for half a day. He always had her time and attention.

We didn't live far from school. That's why we carpooled most days. And I hated to leave my car in the parking lot at school overnight. I'd rather be picked up like a kindergartener than have someone fuck with my ride.

I jumped out of the car and was halfway inside the house before I heard Oz ask if I wanted him to get my bag. Truly, I didn't care. It was my travel bag, and everything I needed to get ready was inside. I was in a hurry because I knew if I wasted a moment, Declan would be here before we left, and I wasn't ready to face him yet.

I took the fastest shower known to man, dried off, and slathered on some lotion before I tied my hair up in a high ponytail. I had no time to dry my hair. It took forever, and I needed to get gone. With my towel wrapped around me, I stepped out of the bathroom and into my room ready to throw on the first thing I saw. Only when I walked inside, the first thing I saw was a pissed off Declan.

TWENTY-TWO

DECLAN

"DO you want to tell me why you sent me *this*?" I held up my phone barely containing the rage and fear that was coursing through my veins. Dani had been avoiding me all morning and I wasn't having any of it. This wasn't middle school. She needed to talk to me.

Wrapping her towel tighter around her slim body, she lifted her chin and squared her shoulders. "Because I can't, okay? Last night we were almost caught, and it was too much. I would be devastated if I got you fired."

"And I would be devastated if I lost you. *You* are seven thousand times more important to me than any stupid job. I'm in no way hurting for money." Would I run out of money eventually? Yes, I would, but I would quit being the coach here in a heartbeat if it meant making things easier for Dani.

Her chin started to wobble. In one smooth move, I reached out and pulled her to me and into my lap. Cradling her in my arms, I kissed the top of her head. "Have we gotten a little reckless? Yes, perhaps we have, but that can be changed. What can't be changed is how much I love you, and how I won't be able to live my life without you in it."

Dani's body shuddered in my hold, and I realized she was crying about one second before I felt the wetness hit my shirt. "Please don't cry, sweetheart. Talk to me, so we can figure this out."

Pushing on my chest, she looked down at the space between us. "I need to get ready. Lo and I have plans."

Lifting her chin with my index finger, I waited until her eyes locked on mine. "I think this is a little more important than a girl's day."

Averting her eyes, she looked over my shoulder. "I need this time, Declan. Please let me have it."

"Are you saying you'll talk to me once you're finished with your day?"

She nodded her head, but I wasn't very convinced. Tightening my hold on her, I knew I needed to give her what she wanted. There was no way I wanted to make her unhappy or feel unsafe with me. "If you don't, we'll end up right where we are now."

Resting her head on my shoulder, she ran one hand

down my back as if to soothe me. Nothing could eliminate the raging beast inside of me until she told me she wasn't ending what we started. "This isn't so bad, is it?"

With the side of my face pressed into her hair, I breathed her in. "It is when I know you're dying to escape, and you're leaving me feeling uncertain about where we're going to end up."

"I love you, Declan. Never doubt my love for you."

How could I not when she made it seem like she was trying to end things between us?

"I love you more than I can ever express. Please talk to me before you make any rash decisions." Kissing the top of her head, I released her and died a little inside at how quickly she escaped my lap.

"I promise we'll talk," she said so quietly I barely heard her as she headed to her closet.

It took everything in me not to throw her down on her bed and fuck her into submission. Remind her how good we were together, but I held back. Barely. Instead, I watched with a heavy heart as she slipped on a pair of shorts underneath a towel and then turned her back to me to pull on a t-shirt.

Looking over her shoulder at me, she at least looked sheepish at hiding her body from me. Dani had never been one to shield herself from me, and seeing her do it now, sent shivers down my spine. Did she hate me for not being able to open with everyone? Was I driving her back into old habits?

"What are your plans today with Lo?"

"We're going to eat a late lunch, get our nails done, and do a little shopping like we used to do before college." She shrugged. "Just getting back to our roots."

I knew how much she missed her friend. I prayed Lo was on my side and would talk some sense into her.

Standing, I forced my hands into my pockets. I was desperate to touch her one last time before I left, but I held back. Now it was me who needed to get out of here before I did something stupid.

"I love you." I proclaimed with every ounce of conviction in my body before I turned around and left her room. I didn't look at a single soul as I left the house and got into my car. The fate of my future was out of my hands and now all I could do was wait.

WIGGLING her toes in the water while we waited to get our nails done, Lo turned to me. "Not that I don't love spending time with you, but what's really going on?"

"Sometimes I hate that you know me so well," I chuckled.

"That's what best friends are for." Her eyes softened as she took me in. "Did something happen between you and Declan? Did he break your heart?"

Not him, but I was thinking of breaking both of our hearts.

"He's been perfect."

Reaching between our seats, she grabbed my hand. "Then why are you having doubts?"

"It's not doubts about him or us, but that we'll be caught. At our last game…" I shook my head at my stupidity and proceeded to tell her everything that happened last night and then today.

"Girl, why are you so against being happy? You probably don't want to hear this, but I'm going to tell it to you anyway. You're practically at Declan's house every night as it is. You should live there and when you have your away games it won't be so difficult to be apart."

Narrowing my eyes at her, I frowned. "Are you saying you would like it if you had to spend a night apart from my brother?"

Lo scoffed and rolled her eyes. "Of course not, but I'd do it for the greater good, and I have done it on his away games. If you don't want him to get fired, you have to make concessions."

"And I what, just tell him I'm moving in or show up on his doorstep with all my belongings in hand?" Now who was being ridiculous?

"He's already offered to let you move in before, and you didn't take him up on it." Tightening her grip on my hand, she smiled sadly. "Listen. I'm not saying it won't be hard to be away from each other on those nights, but the fall season is almost over. You're strong as hell. You can manage a couple of nights away from him."

I wasn't so sure about that. When I was away from Declan, I could barely sleep those nights. I hated how dependent I'd become on him. He was my happiness, and if I didn't have him what would I be?

"And I turned him down. I hurt him today. He didn't say it, but I saw it in his eyes. What if he's done with me?"

"Girl, he loves you. Anyone can see it when he looks at you."

And that's why he doesn't look at me directly when we're at practice or at games.

"I think I need to talk to my therapist."

"That's probably a good idea. And you should talk to Declan. Don't leave him out of what you're feeling."

I knew she was right.

"I love him, Lo, and I don't know what I'd do without him," I confessed.

"Then why are you trying to break up with the poor guy?"

"Because I'm afraid of what will happen if I fall any deeper." Yeah, I was a coward, and I was sabotaging the best thing that ever happened to me. I hated myself for it.

"Do you want to cut our day short, so you can go and talk this out with your man?"

I did and I didn't. I rarely got time where it was only me and my best friend. I cherished our time together.

"Nope, you're stuck with me. We're going to go shopping and get me some crazy, hot lingerie to show

Declan how sorry I am for putting up with me and my craziness."

"He'll be most appreciative. I may have to get me a little something." She flashed me a smile.

"I do not want to think about how you're going to get down with my brother. No thanks." I shivered.

We spent the rest of the afternoon shopping and having fun like the old days. We really needed to do have more days like that more often.

STANDING at his doorway with only a pair of loose-fitting sweatpants, Declan looked down at me with his body tense and his eyes devoid of all emotion. I didn't blame him. He probably thought I was here to end things.

After several seconds of silence, I broke the silence with barely more than a whisper. "Can I come in?"

He didn't say a word as he stepped out of the way and let me walk into his house. My heart started to gallop in my chest. What if Declan was through me and my craziness?

"I'm sorry. I really am." Lifting my head, I was met with the hard lines of his handsome face.

"What are you sorry for?" He wasn't forgiving me so easily this time.

"Everything. For the text message, leaving and not talking to you. But I'm not going to say I'm sorry for worrying about you and how all of this could affect you. Isn't that what you're supposed to do for the person you love?"

Crossing his arms over his bare chest, he gave me nothing. All I knew was he was pissed off and rightfully so. "Tell me right now if this is all too much for you. I don't want to hinder your recovery. I was selfish when I got you back in my life, but I would never be able to live with myself if I was the reason, *again*, for you to become destructive to your own self."

Was he ever going to just see me without worrying about my eating disorder.

"I'm not going to lie and say there aren't time when things become difficult, but that's life. It's not you, it's me. Today I talked to Lo and then went home and talked to my therapist which I should have done *before* I sent that message. And before that I should have talked to you about how I was feeling." Reaching out I took his large hand in my small one. "I freaked out and I'm sorry."

Declan blew out a breath and his body sagged against mine. "You should have talked to me. I've told you time and again that you are what's important to me. I don't care about this job or soccer. I want what's best for you and if that means quitting I will. The fall season is almost over, and maybe Coach Parker can take it back up in the spring. Whatever will make life easier for you."

"I don't want you to give up everything for me, Declan. I still have two years left of school after this. I can't live knowing that you're sitting around waiting for my time."

"Sweet girl," he cupped my cheek. "I wouldn't be sitting around. I can do so much more. I can do soccer camps for the children in the area, and I can host more intensive ones for Olympic hopefuls like yourself."

I loved how he still hadn't given up on my dream even if I had.

"My dream isn't to be a coach for the rest of my life. I can put my degree into use." He smiled down at me. "Stop shutting me out. I'm here to talk through anything you ever need. Even if it's the hard stuff that I don't want to hear."

Pressing forward, I didn't stop until there was no space between us. "So, you're not mad at me?"

"Not at you, but the situation. Imagine how you'd feel if I'd sent you the same text you sent me and then refused to talk to me."

"I'd freak out and cry, and then probably eat an entire pint of ice cream."

"Exactly. Don't put me through that again."

"I won't. Lo had a suggestion that she thought might help." I looked down unsure if I should mention it or how he'd react.

Lifting my chin, the corners of his mouth tipped up. "And what was that?"

"Maybe I would be able to stay away from you when we're at out-of-town games, if I stayed here more permanently."

Damn, I couldn't believe those words just came out of my mouth. Hey, so I don't freak out anymore, why don't I move in? Smooth. Real smooth.

Wrapping his arms around me, he dipped his head until his lips were only millimeters from my own. "I like the sound of that. Is that something you're up for? I don't want to push you."

A laugh burst out of me causing Declan to chuckle. "I'm the one who mentioned it. How are *you* pushing *me*?"

His hands that had come down to rest on my hips flexed. "I don't want you doing this because of what happened last night."

I would never move in if I didn't love him.

"How about because I can't stand the thought of not being in your bed one more night? Or the fact that I love you and I'm hoping to spend the rest of my life with you."

One second my feet were on the floor and the next I was being hoisted in the air as Declan's lips crashed into mine. This wasn't a regular kiss. No, this one screamed possession as he devoured me. It was the single hottest kiss of my life.

When we finally broke for air, I lifted my head to stare into his gorgeous brown eyes that were filled with more love than I ever thought possible.

"I take it you like my reasons?"

He spoke as he walked through the house and into his bedroom. "I more than like, I love it."

Those were the last words we spoke. Wiggling out of his hold, my feet hit the floor and I set about showing Declan how much I loved him.

Slowly I inched my t-shirt up over my stomach. Declan dropped to his knees and kissed every inch of exposed skin. Once I'd felt his touch, I wanted to both rush the process and relish every second to preserve it as one of the most special memories to date. I knew there would be others in our future, but this one would get me through the hard times that would no doubt come.

Inching my shirt up over my breasts, I gasped as Declan's hot mouth took in one nipple and then the other and sucked. His tongue lapped through the lace of my barely there bra.

Ridding myself of my top, I started to push down my shorts only for Declan to rip them down my legs in one smooth move.

My hands gripped his shoulders as he slowly made his way down my body worshiping me in a way that had me feeling breathless.

Hooking a finger through the material that covered my core, he pushed it aside and ran his tongue through my already slick folds.

The moan that came out of his mouth nearly had me combusting on the spot. Two fingers plunged deep inside of me as he lapped at my tiny bundle of nerves. The contrast of his soft tongue compared to the desperate way his fingers moved in and out of me was nearly my undoing.

Fuck he was talented. It took no time at all to bring me over the edge. My legs felt like they were going to go out from under me, but I didn't care. Heat started at the base of my spine and shot straight down to my clit. My body was spilling over with pleasure.

Declan's arm wrapped around me to keep me upright as he slowly brought me down from my extreme high. One second, I was floating in the air and the next, I was resting on his pillowy soft mattress. I wanted to be on my knees with his thick cock in my mouth, but it seemed Declan had other ideas as he kissed and nipped his way up my body. My heart rate had only just started to come down, and was starting to race again.

The passion flowing through his veins was tangible. I surged up at the same time, he plunged deep inside of me. We both let out a collective moan. Lacing his hands through mine, Declan slowly started to rock in and out of me while his lips and tongue tasted every inch he could. My hands roamed the vast planes of his back as his muscles rippled and flexed with each movement. My desire for Declan grew with each passing moment.

Wrapping my legs around his waist with my heels pressed into the firm globes of his ass, I pulled him in deeper. A sharp gasp escaped me as he hit my g-spot over and over again. My hips met each one of his strokes wanting more but not knowing what it was that I wanted or needed.

It wasn't until Declan wrapped his arms around me tightly, and in one quick movement had me straddling him that I got what I needed. Arching my back, I rose and fell on his thick length as one of Declan's hands went to my hip and the other between my legs. The second his callused thumb met my clit; I rode him like a bucking bull.

My body started to quake as fire lit my body from the

base of my spine to the tips of my toes. Placing my hands on Declan's thighs, I arched back. I could feel the tips of my hair caressing my ass before Declan's nails dug into my flesh. He was just as close as I was. The hungry look on his face was more prominent than ever as he gazed up at me. His deep brown eyes burned with lust, and his mouth parted as his breathing grew quicker.

Pinching my clit between two fingers had me coming harder than I'd ever come before in my life. My eyes squeezed shut and white, purple, and yellow dots sparkled behind my lids. My core spasmed in a death grip around his cock. Not only was Declan claiming me, but I was claiming him as well.

Feeling better than I ever had in my entire life, I slumped against Declan's sweaty chest and panted.

With one hand draped low at my hip, the other ran up and down my back. "I love you," he said against my hair, and all was right with the world.

EPILOGUE

Fall
Danica

DECLAN'S THUMB swept across my cheek. Tipping my head in his direction, he smiled at me as he wiped my other cheek.

"I'm so happy." A big smile spread across my face as a few more tears slipped out. "This is the happiest day of my life. So far," I amended. Seeing my brother and best friend get married was a dream. How I ever thought my twin wasn't good enough for Lo was beyond me. Being in a relationship has only made him a better person. Seeing them ecstatic with their wedding bands on their left hands has me thinking about how one day in the future this very well could be me and Declan.

"Good. I like to see you happy."

"I like being happy, and that you're by my side."

"You're never getting rid of me." Running his nose along the column of my neck. His hot breath against his neck sent goosebumps along my skin. "Haven't you learned that yet?"

"I'm starting to get the idea." I already knew, but I liked playing with him. He was my one and only, and we both knew it. I was the clingy one, not him.

Sitting back up, Declan faced back out toward where Oz and Lo were dancing slowly and looking at each other with so much love that if I didn't have Declan in my life, I would have been one jealous bitch. "And what would you think if I asked you to marry me?"

I wasn't sure how I stayed in my seat. If we weren't attending Lo and my brother's wedding, I would have shrieked and jumped up and down.

"Going by the beaming smile across your face and in your eyes, I'm guessing you like the idea."

I wasn't sure if I could wait until I graduated to get married like Lo and Oz did. Granted they didn't have to wait as long.

"Can we get married tomorrow?"

Declan smirked as he kept looking forward. "Is that

what you want? You don't want all of these people at our wedding?"

I wasn't sure what I wanted. All I knew was I didn't want to have to wait two more years.

Unable to help myself, I slid onto his lap and wrapped my arms around Declan's neck. Brushing my nose along his, I pressed my lips to his as I spoke. "Tell me I'm not dreaming."

"It's the best damn dream of my life if it is." Without giving me a chance to answer back, he ran his tongue along the seam of my lips.

This was my life now. All smiles when it came to Declan. "When do you want to get married?"

"I'm with you. Tomorrow is too long to wait, but I want you to have the wedding you've always dreamed about." His hand roamed down my back and along my side.

While Lo had been planning her dream wedding in the fall, all I thought about was having one in the winter. I wanted someplace where the ground was covered in snow with Lo as my maid of honor in a red silk dress. I wasn't sure who would be Declan's best man, but he'd don a red bow tie with his tuxedo. Since Thanksgiving with my family and Friendsgiving with our crew, Declan was becoming fast friends with Oz, Fin, West, Ford, and Xander. We were always at their houses, and they were at ours. I was sure one of them would be his best man. I just wasn't sure which.

"We can get married during winter break. Maybe at Big Bear or Lake Arrowhead." The more I thought about it the more excited I got. "I like the idea of becoming Danica Hart."

"Me too." He grinned. "I want you to have everything your heart desires."

My heart that he was so careful with protecting was about ready to explode in my chest with how much I loved him. "I already have everything I want. I've got you."

"Oh my god, would you two stop? I'm going to ruin my best friend's wedding night by throwing up all over the place," Fin groaned.

"We could keep going or we could talk about when you and West are going to get married," I shot out. There was no way I was going to let Fin ruin my moment.

Fin's mouth clamped shut and his eyes narrowed. I felt bad because while Fin loved the hell out of West, I wasn't sure if he was ready to announce his love to the world.

"Don't bust his balls," Declan said softly enough for only me to hear. He was right, but I wasn't going to let him be an asshole tonight of all nights.

Leaning forward, I clapped my hand over Fin's. "I'm sorry, but tonight's romantic. How can you blame us?"

Fin rolled his black eyes and chuckled. "Tonight, is no different than any other night, and just like those nights, I don't need to see you two making out and looking at each other with stars in your eyes. Leave it for the bedroom."

Ignoring Fin, I rolled my lips as I turned to West. "How do you put up with him?"

Wrapping his arm around Fin's shoulders, West only looked at his boyfriend with love in his eyes. "I guess I'm a masochist because I love his brand of torture."

Oz clamped Fin on the shoulder as he and Lo came to stand behind us. "Who's going to be the next here to get married?"

"Are we taking bets?" Fin clapped his and rubbed them together as he looked us over one at a time. No one answered, but that didn't seem to phase Fin one bit. "It's a tough call between your sister and Ford, but I'm going with little Dani over here."

Oz looked down at me. His blue eyes bright with happiness. "Oh, yeah. Is there something I don't know?"

"Not yet, but maybe soon." Declan's hand on my waist tightened. I wasn't making any plans until after there was a ring on my finger. Absentmindedly, I noticed I was rubbing my left ring finger.

"Soon," Declan whispered in my ear.

"See what I'm talking about?" Fin gestured to me and Declan. "What we should bet on is who will be pregnant first, Dani or Lo?"

I coughed, nearly choking on my tongue. "Listen while the rest of you just graduated, I've still got two more years that I plan to finish, so let's hold off on the talk of babies unless we're talking about me being an aunt."

"I think babies are a little way in the future for us too," Lo said, pressing her hand against her stomach. If her period hadn't been just last week, I would have swore she was pregnant from that gesture alone.

I wasn't in a rush except maybe to have Declan's ring on my finger, but for now I was going to concentrate on finishing up school and my training since I was going to be in the Olympic tryouts, going to as many games as I could of West's since he was drafted to play for the Steelers, and to spend as much time as possible with my man. Life was perfect, and I couldn't ask for anything more. I never thought I would ever be this happy. I was healthy and hadn't had a single relapse thanks to my therapist, Declan, and my friends. I talked to them both about everything, and they made everything manageable. More than that. They made sure I was living my best life every day.

Scooting back from his seat, West pushed up from the table. "What do you all say we get a drink before Fin, and I have to catch our flight?"

Oz gripped West on the shoulder. "Thanks for making the trip. I know how busy you are, and that you choose to come here on your day off before a game."

"I wouldn't miss today for anything." They did some awkward, weird man hug that had me and Lo looking at each other with big grins on our faces.

Wrapping Lo in my arms, I hugged her harder than I'd ever hugged her before. "I'm sorry I ever thought you and Oz shouldn't be together. I've never seen you as happy as you are right now. It kills me that I tried to keep you apart."

"It's alright." She sniffed in my ear. "I won't hold it against you. I know you were just looking out for my best interest. Don't let these little things eat at you." Pulling back, Lo cupped my cheeks. "We're all happy, and that's amazing. Declan looks at you with so much love in his eyes." Gripping my arm, she pulled me away from the table a few feet away. An almost embarrassed smirk crossed her face. "When you brought Declan to Friendsgiving the first time, I… I wasn't a fan. He was so intense and strange, but now I know he was already in love with you. I'm glad you two worked your way back together. I love seeing you happy."

"I'm so happy. I can't believe he's stayed with me and my craziness," I admitted the last part quietly.

"He's never going to leave your side. I'm surprised you don't have a ring on your finger yet."

Leaning in closer so she could hear me over the music, I could barely contain my giddiness. "He kind of asked me earlier."

Lo's eyes went wide and then went to my bare ring finger. "Where's the ring?"

My eyes darted to where Declan stood by the bar with my brother and our friends. I guess they were going to have that drink without us. "It's not official yet. He asked what I'd say like there's any possibility of any other answer but yes."

"Eek," Lo shrieked. Luckily no one could hear her. I was sure they'd be wondering what the hell was going on with us. I didn't want my parents to know yet. They would have my wedding planned before the ring was on my finger. "I'm so excited for you."

"Me too," I beamed at her.

"We should probably get over there before West and Fin have to leave." Her bottom lip stuck out. "I wish they could stay longer, but I know how difficult it was for West to work this into his schedule."

"They wouldn't have missed it for the world."

Looping my arm through hers, we set off across the floor to the bar.

"When do you think they'll get married?" She asked as we walked up. Oz instantly had her in his arms.

"As soon as Fin gets his head out of his ass."

Fin narrowed his eyes at me while everyone else laughed even though they had no idea what we were talking about.

"Why are you on my case?" He frowned at me.

"Because I love you."

Fin's eyes widened as he took a step back. West pulled him back into our circle laughing.

"Like a brother." I shivered at the thought of anything else.

His brows furrowed. "I know," he said gruffly.

"How about one more shot before we have to say goodbye?" West offered.

The bartender already had eight shot glasses lined up and ready for us. I wasn't sure what was inside, but I didn't care. All of our lives were changing, and I wasn't sure when I'd see most of them again. Ford and Xander were thinking of moving down to LA, so Ford could work in some fancy restaurant there, while Lo and Oz were moving to San Diego for their new jobs. While they wouldn't be far, I wouldn't be able to drive a few minutes to see them whenever I wanted.

Lifting our shot glasses, Fin toasted. "To a life full of happiness, and to Lo not getting pregnant on your honeymoon."

Lo coughed and sputtered for a few seconds before she drank down her shot.

It wasn't long before we were saying goodbye to Fin and West with tears in our eyes, or at least me and Lo were close to crying.

"We can FaceTime anytime you want," West called from the Uber they'd just stepped into.

It wasn't true since we all had busy schedules, but it was a nice gesture. Next it was Oz and Lo's turn to head to their hotel room to kickstart their honeymoon. They were spending a week in Hawaii before they came back and moved.

"I guess that leaves us," Ford said, as we stood and watched the newlyweds drive off with the rest of the crowd.

"I guess so," Declan muttered as he stood behind me with his arms wrapped around my waist.

"We'll have to get together before we move down to LA," Xander added.

"Damn, I'm going to miss you and your cooking." I hugged Ford. "But I know you're going to do amazing with your internship, and it will be no time at all before you're opening up your very own restaurant and we'll be lucky to get a table."

"You'll always have a table in any restaurant I'm in." Ford hugged me back and then did some weird handshake with Declan. "I don't know about you, but I'm ready to get out of here."

I was, but I knew I had to say goodbye to my parents first. They were dead on their feet, but they had the biggest smiles on their faces as they came toward us.

"It's almost time," Declan whispered in my ear as he moved around to my side right before my parents stepped in front of us.

"Please tell me we have at least a year before the two of you get married," my mom said with an exhausted smile. She was a tiny woman compared to the rest of us, but the most beautiful woman I'd ever seen. Her blonde hair was cut short into a bob and her blue eyes radiated so much happiness.

"I can promise you; I won't get married until I'm finished with school. One thing at a time."

"Good," my father laughed, giving my mom a side hug. "I've barely seen your mom in the last two months. I can't lose her again so quickly."

My mom had become a bit of a mother-in-law-zilla. While Lo didn't love it, I was all for my mother planning my wedding. It was a hell of a lotta work. It also helped that I knew exactly what I wanted after helping the two of them, but that was all in good time.

"Does that mean I have your permission to ask for your daughter's hand in marriage?" Declan asked, stepping up to my dad.

My heart swelled in my chest as the gesture. I knew it meant a lot to my dad for Declan to ask him.

"If you promise to keep treating her like a princess then yes," my dad laughed and shook Declan's hand.

"I'll do more than that. Once we're married, I'm going to treat your daughter like a queen."

"That's what I like to hear." My mom leaned into my dad's side, and he shifted to put his arm around her. "We should probably get out of here before I have to carry your mom. I guess we'll see you at Thanksgiving."

"If not sooner." I missed my parents and with everyone moving away, I had a feeling I'd want to see them more. It was nice that they weren't as worried about me anymore. I'd put on most of the weight I'd lost, and I wasn't self-conscious about the way I looked any longer. Declan was a big help in that department. He was always reassuring me I was beautiful. Between him and talking to my therapist once a week, I was better than ever. At least in my opinion. I was open and honest with my feelings instead of keeping them bottled up and then reacting in the worst of ways.

Dipping his head down until his forehead rested on mine, Declan's eyes twinkled from the fairy lights that were strewn around the area and in the trees. "What do you say we go home and practice for our honeymoon?"

Tipping my head up until our lips met, I smiled against his soft, full lips. "I can't think of anything I'd like more."

The End.

Want more? Me too! I'm not ready to let go of these characters. I love them so much. I have more planned for them. This won't be the last time you see the Willow Bay gang. I also plan to write a generation two set in Willow Bay with their siblings and others.

Did you enjoy OFF SIDES If so, please consider leaving a review on Goodreads, Amazon, or BookBub. Reviews mean the world to authors especially to authors who are starting out. You can help get your favorite books into the hands of new readers.

I'd appreciate your help in spreading the word and it will only take a moment to leave a quick review. It can be as short or as long as you like. Your review could be the deciding factor or whether or not someone else buys my book.

To stay up to date on all my releases subscribe to my newsletter. https://ellakade.com/newsletter/

ACKNOWLEDGMENTS

My family- your support means so much. Thank you for all of your encouragement and giving me the time to do what makes me happy.

Thank you **Bex** for making my story into a book.

To all my **author friends**, you know who you are. Thank you for accepting me and making me feel welcome in this amazing community.

To **Wildfire Marketing Solutions and Catherine**, thank you for all your knowledge and for helping me make Away Game a success!

Lovers thank you for always being there.

To each and every **reader**, **reviewer**, and **blogger** - I would be nowhere without you. Thank you for taking a chance on an unknown author.

ABOUT ELLA

Ella Kade is a forbidden and dark romance writer who enjoys writing captivating characters with sinful intent.

Read Ella to get immersed into her words where she ruins lives and slowly puts them back together.

ALSO BY ELLA KADE

<u>Willow Bay Series - Forbidden Romance</u>

Away Game - MM, Bully

First Down - Sister's Best Friend

Over Time - MM, Student/Teacher

Off Sides - Second Chance, Forbidden

Sin's Sacrifice - MC, Second Chance

King's Vow - Secret Society, Drug Cartel, Bodyguard, Reverse Age Gap - December 12, 2022